All Other Perils

By

Alex Clifford

All Other Perils
Copyright © 2009 by
Alex Clifford

Library of Congress Catalog Card Number – Pending

First Printing

Published by

Cogwheel Press
P.O. Box 9592
Ketchikan, AK 99901

For a personalized copy order directly from

Cogwheelpress.com

ISBN: 978-0-578-00705-2

Acknowlegments

I want to thank my wife, Jennifer, for putting up with all my outrageous stunts and near death experiences. I would also like to thank the doctors and nurses at Saint Patrick's Hospital for bringing me back from the brink so I could finish this book. Special thanks go to the nurses in the fifth floor Neurological Ward for the way they babied me back to health.

Disclaimer

Look for other books by
Alex Clifford
along with other titles at
www.newonlinebooks.com

Do not wear yourself out to get rich:
have the wisdom to show restraint.
Cast but a glance at riches and they are gone,
for they will surely sprout wings
and fly off to the sky like an eagle.

Proverbs 23:4-5

1

There's a scar along my left jaw where some lowlife in Mexico tried to cut my throat but missed my jugular by a couple of inches. An emergency room medic in Hermosillo stitched me up and when I got home, my doctor in Huntington Beach said I'd need plastic surgery, but when the gash finally healed, it left nothing more than a razor-thin line from below my mouth to a spot underneath my left ear. The doctor told me I was lucky because I was the kind of person that scarred on the inside. He had no idea how right he was. The scar tissue itches sometimes, a peculiar cutting sensation like a knife slicing flesh, white-hot at times, and it's deep under my skin where I can't scratch it. Lately I've noticed it acts up when there's trouble brewing, and tonight, that itch went clean to the bone.

It was Tuesday evening and I was sitting in my office at the Coast Guard's Terminal Island base trying to catch up on paperwork. As the Officer-in-Charge of Port Security for San Pedro Harbor, I'd spent the last week back in Washington for a series of meetings, conferences, and presentations with the Department of Homeland Security. The highlight of my trip was the testimony I'd given before a Congressional sub-committee in regards to West Coast maritime security risks and then I'd asked them for more funding for the Eleventh Coast Guard District. My jurisdiction, the southern part of the Eleventh District headquartered up the coast in Alameda, consisted of over three hundred miles of California coastline from Point Conception to the Mexican border and it kept me as busy as a one-legged man in an ass-kicking contest. When I got back from Washington a few hours ago, my desk was strewn with reports of suspicious floating objects, overdue yachts, fishing boat violations, merchant vessel infractions, weird lights in the sky, harbor radiation detector readings, and a lot of other files that I suspected wound up on my desk just because I was gone and people didn't what else to do with them.

My cell phone rang just as I finished reading the incident report about the thirty-eight foot Bertram sportfisher named *Lemon Twist* that went aground on the San Pedro breakwater. The report concluded alcohol had been a factor. How about that?

I checked the incoming call and recognized it as San Pedro Homicide Detective Rachel Terazzo's official work cell phone so I punched the green button and said hello.

"Commander Stanton?"

"I've only been gone a week," I said. "You can still call me Jared." I wondered why she was being so formal because we'd been on a first name basis for the past several months. Rachel worked the night shift as a homicide detective and a fair number of dead bodies had been turning up around the harbor lately. We'd had coffee about a dozen times and breakfast once or twice.

"I've got something you might want to take a look at," she said.

"What's that?" I asked.

"A body."

"Yours?" As soon as I said it, I made a face and wished I could somehow reach into the phone and retrieve the asinine remark. I attributed it to extreme lack of sleep this past week. That, and too many Red Bulls that I used to chase down the little white happy pills my shrink prescribed to tweak my perception of reality back into the normal range.

There was an awkward pause and I started to apologize but she said, "You ain't that lucky."

There were other people talking in the background over her cell phone. "Where are you?" I asked.

"Berth Ninety-Four in San Pedro."

"Whose body?"

"The Chief Engineer on the *Balboa Victory*."

"The *Balboa Victory*?" I knew the ship but didn't know it had a Chief Engineer already. Two weeks earlier the *Balboa Victory* had been dead-towed down the coast from the U.S Maritime Administration's fleet of mothballed merchant ships it kept in Suisun Bay near San Francisco. MARAD was finally culling what was known as the West Coast 'Ghost Fleet', and since the *Balboa*

Victory had been built during World War Two when the strategy was to build ships faster than German and Japanese torpedoes could sink them, she had been obsolete for decades. The *Balboa Victory* was a sister-ship to the *Dixie Victory*, a museum ship presently operating out of San Pedro by the Merchant Marine Veteran's Association, a loosely formed group of over-the-hill merchant seamen trying to recapture something they'd lost long ago. The Veteran's Association had acquired the *Dixie Victory* about ten years ago and restored her to pristine original condition. Now they'd wrestled the *Balboa Victory* from MARAD's grasp and intended to restore the ship to her former glory as a veteran of three wars: World War Two, Korea and Vietnam.

"What happened?" I asked.

"That's what we're trying to figure out," she said. "But that isn't why I'm calling."

"Then why are you calling?"

"There's something weird going on here," she said, her voice no more than a whisper now. I could hear more talking in the background again. "I just thought you might want to know about it. Come if you want, I gotta go."

"I'll be there in ten minutes," I said, but she was already gone.

I leaned back in my chair, popped several vertebrae in my neck, and then looked at my watch. It was eight-forty already.

"What the hell's going on now?" I muttered. The Port of San Pedro encompasses 7,500 acres, 43 miles of waterfront, and 26 cargo terminals that handled dry and liquid bulk cargo, containers, automobiles and passengers for the over 6,000 ships that visited the port every year. A lot of bizarre things happen in this harbor, especially at night, and suddenly my scar tingled like never before. I pulled the bottle of little white happy pills from my pant's pocket, shook it three or four times so it would make that familiar 'rattlesnake' sound, popped the cap, dropped one of the small oval tablets into my palm, and then swallowed it dry.

I hadn't eaten since breakfast because of my hectic day and was starving. A row of vending machines was strategically positioned by the back door on my way to the parking lot and I shoved most of my loose change into a couple of them. A can of Pepsi dropped with a thud, the sound reverberating up and down the empty hallways of the Coast Guard building, the arrival of the Snickers somewhat quieter. Armed with proper nutrition, I shoved the back door open and stepped into the night. Typical of June weather in Southern California, a strong marine layer was building; bringing fog to the coastal areas that wouldn't burn off until early tomorrow afternoon. As I walked to my car, I peeled the wrapper from the candy bar and took a bite, the taste of nuts and caramel were in my mouth but the pelagic aroma of harbor fog and the stench from the nearby Pacific Fish Company sardine cannery filled my nostrils.

The sentry leaned out the window of the security shack and saluted me off the Coast Guard base, noting the license number of my generic blue government sedan on his clipboard as I left. I made a left turn onto Seaside Avenue and drove cautiously through the gray murk past the working container terminals, nibbling on my Snickers and sipping the can of Pepsi that I kept cradled between my legs as I headed toward the Vincent Thomas Bridge. The 6,000-foot long bridge arcs 185 feet above the ship channel and just before I was halfway across, I climbed above the fog. To my left, the deck lights of a cargo ship at Berth 230 rose above the fog layer, eerily illuminating the silvery veil that concealed the deck of the ship and the turbid waters of the ship channel below. A truck carrying a Yang Ming Line shipping container across the bridge the other way honked his horn, signaling that I had wandered into his lane. I dropped what was left of my candy bar somewhere on the floorboard and swerved as truck tires flashed past my side window. A surge of adrenalin mingled with my emerging sugar high. On the other side of the bridge, I descended back into the fog, riding the brakes so I wouldn't drive past the right hand exit for Harbor Boulevard. The exit ramp circled around under the bridge and when there was a gap in the traffic, I ran the red light and pulled into the parking lot at Berth 94.

The parking lot could hold about forty cars on a busy day and had been recently repaved, indicated by its smooth black surface and the acrid smell of new asphalt emanating from the sedan's dash air vents. Even though the parking spaces were clearly marked with fresh white paint, six black and white SPPD cruisers as well as several unmarked cars were parked helter-skelter around the *Balboa Victory*'s gangway without regard to the neat white lines. The coroner's van was camped out at the base of the gangway where a uniformed police officer stood guard while wolfing down a meatball sandwich he clutched in one fist.

"Follow the yellow tape," he said, motioning me up the gangway with a sideways gesture of his head, his mouth full of food as he spoke.

"What the fuck is the Coast Guard doing here?" said a voice from the shadows to my left.

I walked toward the voice and within a few steps scented cigar smoke.

"I'm Commander Stanton, Port Security," I said to the bulky man leaning his buttocks against one of the unmarked cars. The glow of the cigar in the corner of his mouth betrayed his facial features. As I drew nearer, I could see he was built like a fireplug with a high Neanderthal brow and narrow eyes. He wore a dark windbreaker with his blue jeans. I offered to shake hands but he just stared at me. We stood in silence until he blew smoke in my direction.

"Cuban," I said. "Nice."

I don't smoke cigars, but my father had been a cigar aficionado and I'd spent years in South Florida where fine cigars are a religion. I stepped closer and could see he was smoking a Churchill and then I recognized the unique aroma of the Cohiba, rumored to be Fidel Castro's personal choice.

"So what the fuck is the Coast Guard doing here?" he asked again, his tone a little more hostile this time. "This doesn't concern you."

"Like I said, I'm with Port Security and we got a call about a body on this ship. I'm here to find out what happened."

"We've got it covered, Commander," he said, waving his cigar in my direction. "Go home to your family. It's late, we'll make sure you get a copy of our report."

"I didn't catch your name." I knew quite a few of the San Pedro detectives but I'd never seen this guy before. But then again, SPPD had a lot of new faces and shuffled them around a lot.

The stranger puffed on his cigar again and when he exhaled he said, "Give me your card and I'll see you get a copy of our report."

I dug a card from my uniform pocket and handed it to him.

"Thanks, I'd appreciate a copy of that report." I turned to leave. "I'm going to take a quick look at what's going on here."

"You're fucking funeral, Commander," he said. "Your best bet is to go home to your family and stay the fuck out of our business."

I turned back to face him. He was sucking on the Cohiba as he stared at me. I nodded and resumed walking towards the ship.

My scar itched like crazy and I had the nagging feeling that I should have listened to him, but Rachel Terazzo had called me so I felt I should at least show up to find out why. As I walked toward the ship I wondered how much the SPPD was paying their detectives these days. Was it enough to afford Cuban cigars that went for seventy-five bucks a pop?

2

The *Balboa Victory* lurked in the fog like a grizzled derelict behemoth, her bow and stern barely visible in the fog, the aged battleship-gray paint damp and rusty. The midship gangway was steep and poorly lit with a large black cable running up it to the deck of the ship. A passing sea-bound tugboat with a fuel barge in tow caused the ship to surge under her slackened mooring lines as I stepped aboard. The ship was dead. In maritime terms, that meant she wasn't providing her own power from onboard generators, but instead, drawing SoCal Edison electricity via the heavy black cable running up the gangway. Nobody had bothered to switch on the vessel's deck lighting so I struggled to follow the yellow tape with only the fog-filtered glow from the parking lot for illumination. It occurred to me that a flashlight would have been handy.

The yellow tape led me to a cumbersome watertight door designed to keep the sea from entering the superstructure when the ship was underway. The door was crusty with corrosion and groaned on its decayed hinges when I pulled it open. I stepped into the narrow fore and aft passageway on the main deck of the crew's quarters, and once inside the ship, I found the lights had been turned on. The passageway was painted a tepid pea-green and the steel deck underfoot was shiny mahogany red. The air inside the ship smelled old, decades old, and reeked of fuel oil, grease and wet paint. I followed the yellow tape down the passageway past padlocked cabin doors until I came to a junction. The tape went left, down the wider main cross-passageway in the crew's quarters. Halfway down the passageway, on the forward bulkhead, I found the bronze builder's plate, a two-foot wide oval monument that showed the ship had been built in the California Shipyard in San Pedro as Victory Ship hull number seventy-two and launched on June 12th, 1944. She had a length overall of 445 feet and a beam of 63 feet. Her loaded draft was 28 feet and her deadweight was 10,850 long tons. Next to the builder's plate, under glass, was a faded and decaying general arrangement plan for the ship. It showed the crew's quarters and engine room amidships with three cargo holds being forward and two cargo holds aft. Each cargo hold was divided vertically into upper 'tween deck, lower 'tween deck, and lower hold.

Across the passageway from the builder's plate, the yellow tape went down a stairway that went aft and then at a large landing, went forward again. The tape led through another watertight door into the upper 'tween deck of number three cargo hold.

The body was illuminated with portable battery powered lights and Rachel Terazzo stood about twenty feet away from it. Her chestnut hair was pulled back into a short ponytail and she was wearing gray wool slacks, comfortable but clunky black work shoes, and a lined navy-blue SPPD windbreaker that was two sizes too big so it could cover the Colt Python .357 Magnum she wore cross-draw on her left hip.

Lieutenant Rodney Richards, Rachel's boss who I sometimes knew on a first name basis, depending on his mood, was closer to the body and talking to someone from the coroner's office. Lieutenant Richards was a small black man with long slender fingers, closely cropped hair, and an annoyed expression that had become permanent years ago.

As my vision adjusted to the weak illumination in the otherwise pitch-black cargo hold, I saw scores of wooden and steel boxes stacked to various heights in groups around the cargo hold. More people were standing in the shadows, some were uniformed officers and others wore plain street clothes. Given the circumstances, I didn't want to give it away that Rachel had called me so I didn't say anything as I walked between her and Lieutenant Richards to look at the body.

"What the hell are you doing here?" snapped Lieutenant Richards when he noticed me.

"The Coast Guard has paperwork, too, you know," I said. "Anytime somebody gets killed on one of these ships we have to file a report."

Lieutenant Richards gave me due consideration with coal black eyes for a moment and then resumed murmuring to the guy in the coroner's jacket, adjusting his stance so he could watch me.

"Hey," I said softly, drawing closer to Rachel.

"Hey," she said back, her cinnamon eyes smiling. "Glad you made it."

Rachel Terazzo was Brooklyn Italian. She'd gone to Rutgers, letting the National Guard pay her college tuition. Her plans to attend law school got sidetracked when her unit was deployed to Iraq. She did seventeen months with the Military Police in Baghdad and when she finally came home she'd taken a wrong turn somewhere, ending up in San Pedro instead of Brooklyn. She did a little beach time to clear her head, but when her money ran out she looked for a job. Because of her military experience, the San Pedro Police Department snagged her and as soon as she graduated from their academy, they put her undercover with the vice squad. Rachel had that rare combination of sweet 'girl next door' looks and toughened street smarts. She was twenty-eight years old and tough as nails, but could pass for sweet sixteen with a little makeup. Unfortunately for her, she ended up working undercover in the harbor's rampant porn industry. When her squad cracked a ring making teenage snuff films, some of her soft-core porn pictures ended up the grocery store tabloids from San Diego to Hoboken. Cruelly dubbed the 'Hooker Cop', her undercover days were over and now she was working nights on homicide until things cooled down for her or she found a better gig.

"Who is he?" I asked. The gray-haired man, stomach down on the steel deck, wore oil smudged khakis and heavy steel-toed work boots. His head was awkwardly twisted to the left and his legs were straight with his toes pointed back. Not a lot of blood, just a small pool under his head.

"James Wierman," she said.

"He's old," I said. "Maybe it was a heart attack or stroke and he hit his head when he fell."

"Drag marks." Rachel clicked on her flashlight and the let the beam fall on the drag path left in the grime on the steel deck. "And his car's missing from the parking lot."

I stepped closer and could smell her lavender body wash. "What's going on?" I asked in a lower voice.

She pointed with her eyes to two guys in the shadows. They both looked like college football players. The African-American one had shoulder length dreadlocks and wore a white muscle shirt that showed off what had to be steroid enhanced biceps and deltoids. The blonde one was just as substantially put together and wore a blue flowered Hawaiian shirt that gave him that beach boy surfer look. The dank chill in the cargo hold was starting to give me goose bumps, but these two clowns were dressed for the tropics.

"Who are they?"

"They're with the Agency."

"The Agency?" My mind struggled. Employment agency? Did the Veteran's

Association use an employment agency to get workers for their ship?   I thought they used volunteer labor. "Which agency?"

"The Agency...CIA."

"What?"

She shrugged, her eyes said, "That's what I'm talking about."

I stepped closer and could smell her warmth. "This isn't CIA jurisdiction," I said. "As a matter of fact, they're not even supposed to be operating domestically."

Rachel nodded agreement.   "They want the body."

"You're kidding?   Why would they want the body?"

She shrugged again and looked over at her boss.   "That's what he's talking to the coroner about. He's not going to let them have it."

I looked back at the corpse on the deck and tried to figure out what there was about James Wierman that would interest the Central Intelligence Agency. Who was this guy?

"There's more," Rachel said.

"What?"

"The FBI is here, too."

"What are they doing here?   Did you call them?"

"That's what's weird," she said. "We didn't call anybody, they just showed up, and now the CIA wants to take the body."

Actually, it wasn't too much of a stretch for the FBI to be involved. After all, the ship had belonged to the U.S. Maritime Administration and a murder aboard an American ship would be within their jurisdiction. However, it was unusual for them to want to be involved in something as mundane as a dead merchant seaman, especially with so many other high-profile national security issues these days. Normally, we'd have to beg them to show up on something like this. But the CIA was another matter; they shouldn't be here at all. Besides, the two guys standing in the shadows didn't look like they came out of any standard CIA mold I'd ever seen.

"Jared Stanton," said a voice from the shadows. "How the hell are you?"

I turned to face a man dressed in an expensive waist length black leather jacket, white button down oxford shirt and blue jeans. He had neatly trimmed hair, a pleasant round face and hazel eyes. It took me moment to recognize Lloyd Waller. He wasn't dressed in the FBI's standard dark suit and tie so it was obvious that he'd been called from home on short notice.

"It's been a few years," Lloyd said, as we shook hands.

"Yes, it has," I said. "Good to see you again."

Waller and I worked together briefly when I did my four and a half year stint with the FBI. My late wife, Elisha had been complaining about the sea time I was racking up in the Coast Guard and wanted me closer to home so we could start a family. The FBI was recruiting and liked my background- Coast Guard Academy, drug enforcement, dealing with the Cuba refugee crisis, and a few other qualifications I'd loaded on my resume. Waller and I went to the FBI Academy at the same time and ended up on a special operations task force together after graduation. Since I was working out of Washington D.C., Elisha and I bought a small house near Prince Frederick, Maryland and got busy trying to have kids. Things went good for a few months and then my rabbi, Bureau-speak for mentor, the head of my task force that took me under his wing to develop my career, died unexpectedly of a heart attack at the ripe old age of fifty-two.

"I heard you went back to the Coast Guard after the Boca incident," Lloyd said.

Shortly after my rabbi died, typical Bureau back-biting politics took over and after my position was eliminated, I was shuffled off to an undercover operation based in Boca Raton. The Boca assignment that was responsible for my marriage ending up in disaster, the bottle of happy pills in my pocket, and the weekly sessions with a shrink to discuss my dreams.

"They made me an offer I couldn't refuse." I didn't really want to talk about Boca so I changed the subject. "Why is the Bureau involved in this?"

"Routine procedure," Lloyd said with an FBI issued poker face.

Sometimes you ask questions you already know the answer to and sometimes you just go fishing. In only two words, Lloyd Waller told me his presence here tonight was anything but routine.

Turning back to Rachel I asked, "How'd you find the body?"

She pointed to a hobbled up senior citizen talking to one of the SPPD uniformed officers securing the scene. "His name is Frank Burch.

He's with the Merchant Marine Veterans and works down the dock on the *Dixie Victory*. When Wierman didn't come home, his wife called Frank and asked him to find her husband and tell him dinner was ready. Frank found the body, called 911, a patrol unit came down to take a look, and then called us in when they found the drag marks."

I looked over at Frank Burch and listened to what he was saying to the uniformed officer.

"I'm telling you this ship is haunted," Frank Burch said, spittle forming in the corners of his mouth. "Three men were killed right here in this cargo hold in June of 1970."

The uniformed officer tried to act like he was listening to Frank's story, but his facial expression said he'd heard it several times already. Frank Burch was bug-eyed, with the edgy and scattered look of a man that had way too many synapses firing in his brain.

"They were hauling bombs to Vietnam when they hit the typhoon. Bombs were rolling around down here like loose marbles," Frank Burch babbled, waving his hands to indicate how the bombs moved. "This ship is haunted, I told them not to bring this ship back to San Pedro, bad things were going to happen, and look at what's happened already. Those guys were killed right here where we're standing, right here in this cargo hold and the government knew those bombs hadn't been stowed to specifications and they didn't do a damn thing about it."

Lieutenant Richards finished his conversation with the official from the coroner's office and made a beeline for the two CIA men.

"I'm telling you right now," Lieutenant Richards said, poking the dreadlocked CIA agent in the chest with a finger. "Stay away from that body, this is my jurisdiction, and if you pull any funny shit, I swear to God I'll hunt you two down like dogs and kick your asses myself!"

Lieutenant Richards looked over at me and I was scratching my jaw. The itch was getting worse.

Rachel was listening to her boss and I nudged her to get her attention. "What's with the asshole in the parking lot who's smoking a Cuban cigar?"

Rachel's expression told me she didn't know what I was talking about.

"Stocky guy, high forehead, smokes seventy-five dollar Cohibas," I said. "He made it sound like he was with San Pedro P.D. and said he send me a copy of your report."

Rachel shook her head. "He's not one of ours."

3

Rachel Terazzo was right. Something weird was going on aboard the *Balboa Victory*. But ultimately, it didn't concern me. Lieutenant Rodney Richards could argue with the Agency and the Bureau about who was going to take possession of the body until he was blue in the face for all I cared. I wanted no part of it. In due course, someone associated with the *Balboa Victory* would have to file a report with the Coast Guard Marine Safety Office concerning the death of James Wierman, but that was a different office and I'd never even see the report. So while the presence of the CIA and FBI aboard the *Balboa Victory* tonight was puzzling, it really was none of my business. I didn't know what they were up to, but I was familiar enough with how they operated that I wasn't going to stick my nose into their affairs if I didn't have to.

Besides, I had other priorities, and right now, I wanted to get down to the Harbor Light before the kitchen closed. I hadn't eaten a decent meal all day and Tuesday was Cajun Prime Rib Sandwich night. They served dinner until eleven o'clock and if I hurried, I still might be able to get a sandwich before they sold out.

The Harbor Light sat on the corner of 4th Street and Harbor Boulevard in San Pedro, a short hop from the *Balboa Victory* and directly across the street from China Shipping's container terminal. There was a parking spot on 4th Street about halfway up the block so I wedged the government sedan between a fairly new gray Buick four-door and a red extended-cab Toyota pickup. A set of headlights came out of the fog from somewhere up 4th Street and I waited for the car to clear me before I jaywalked and headed for Harbor Boulevard. When I rounded the corner I saw Reverend Johnny, a local vagrant and preacher of the gospel, plying his trade on the sidewalk. He was wearing a set of ragged Army fatigues and sitting on a plastic five-gallon bucket while strumming his guitar and jamming to the music blasting from a boom-box. All his worldly possessions were in a shopping cart that had a cardboard sign on the side of it advertising 'VIETNAM VET-WILL WORK FOR FOOD' in large black letters, and in smaller lettering, 'Jesus loves you!' done in artsy-fartsy rainbow colors. I stuck two bucks in his coffee can when I walked past but he didn't acknowledge me.

As I pushed my way through the front door of the restaurant, the humid fragrance of roasted chicken and freshly baked dinner rolls rushed past me to merge with the mist-laden night air on the sidewalk. There weren't a lot of diners at a quarter to ten; the big rush was usually earlier in the evening. The sign said 'Please Wait To Be Seated', but the hostess wasn't around and I ducked into the cozy bar area to the left.

"Look what the cat dragged in." Stan was the Harbor Light's bartender and he flashed me the same grin all the regulars get when they arrive.

The corner seat of the L-shaped bar was open so I took it. There were four other patrons in the bar hovered over their drinks. Nobody I knew. They looked over at me as I sat down and the lone neon Corona beer sign on the wall behind me made their eyes look pink.

Stan poured a double shot of Jack Daniels over a highball glass full of ice, popped the tab on a can of diet 7-Up and set both on the bar in front of me. He was going to let me mix the Jack and Seven to my own specifications.

"I haven't seen you in awhile," he said.

Stan was an affable sort of average build with dark neatly trimmed hair and a horsey smile that was too big for his face. He tugged at the black bow tie that interfered with his Adam's apple. His white long-sleeved shirt and black pants were clean and neatly pressed, as per standing orders from the Harbor Light's new management.

"I've been out of town," I said, pouring a little 7-Up into the glass and poking at the ice cubes to blend it with the sour mash. I took a sip and then added a little more mixer.

"That's right, I remember now," he said, wiping at the bar with a towel. "You said you were going back East."

"Do they have enough prime rib left to make another sandwich?"

"I'll check." Stan ducked under the bar at the far end and disappeared into the kitchen.

I played with the ice cubes in my glass and avoided eye contact with the other customers. My mind drifted back to the cigar-smoking stranger in the parking lot. Why had he warned me away from the case? He'd said, "Your fucking funeral, Commander." I scratched my scar. Nothing made sense.

"It's on the way," Stan said, tugging the bow tie even looser.

"Thanks. Where's Beverley?" Odds were that Beverley wasn't around tonight because Stan's tie wouldn't be loose if she was. Beverley, a local real estate agent with questionable scruples, was the new part-owner and manager of the Harbor Light as well as the favorite topic of conversation in the bar these days.

"I heard somebody say that she went over to Catalina Island," he said, wiping at imaginary spots on the bar with his white towel. "Some sort of business deal, but she doesn't check in and out with me."

The Jack and Seven was mixed just right and I swallowed a healthy dose, the whiskey burning all the way to my stomach. "Any news about the sale of this place?"

Stan smiled like a Cheshire cat. It was a local joke. The Harbor Light had been known as The Tropics bar fourteen months ago and sat on the same piece of property as the Hotel Savoy next door. The legendary Southern California real estate developer Ernest Waddell had owned the property until his death. In some sort of cruel family prank, Ernest Waddell left the property, currently valued at over a hundred million dollars, to a dozen or so of his heirs, making them instant millionaires. The only catch was that all the heirs had to come to an agreement on what to do with the property. Some wanted to sell right away to get their money, others wanted to roll the dice and play the skyrocketing real estate game. Bitter family fighting broke out and several restraining orders were issued before Beverley was finally able to establish some sort of peace by convincing everyone they would double their money in a couple of years by waiting for the right buyer. The port was expanding by leaps and bounds she had told them, but no new real estate was being created. Be patient.

The pink eyes in the bar turned in my direction as six merchant seamen entered the Harbor Light. They looked to be Korean and the first one through the door stopped suddenly, the others bumping into him in a comical chain reaction. I could tell by their expressions that the place had changed quite a bit since the last time they were here. The tallest one asked Stan a question in broken English, his words unintelligible through a thick accent, but really there was little interpreting to be done. They had the peckish look of men that had spent the last several months aboard ship between the devil and the deep blue sea and were now ready to cash in a few of their hard earned fun coupons.

"No girls." Stan said.

After a few moments of confusion and whispering, they pushed their way back to the street. The pink eyes at the bar re-focused on their drinks.

Until Beverley took over The Tropics, it had been a run down seaman's bar serving flat beer, cheap whiskey, and hot and cold running hookers. The Hotel Savoy next door had rooms that went for six hundred dollars a night, usually rented out for fifty bucks an hour. After you paid for your room in cash at the front desk, you got a room key, one sheet, one towel, and a small bar of soap. Or so I heard.

A little over a year ago, as part owner and self-appointed leader of the heirs, Beverley put herself on the payroll as manager, took out a mortgage using the property as collateral, then contracted for a multi-million dollar renovation of The Tropics and Savoy Hotel that was done in Nouveaux California Chic. Rumor had it that Beverley was sleeping with the contractor and getting cash kickbacks on all his work. We all figured it was just a matter of time until the heirs started bumping each other off.

I wasn't sure what Nouveaux California Chic was, other than mirrors and ferns, but I did know that the Harbor Light didn't smell like urine and vomit anymore, and that the kitchen was clean with plenty of hot food at a reasonable price.

The first drink slid right down my throat and when I caught Stan's eye I tipped my glass, signaling him to hit me again. The girl at the pharmacy that puts those little stickers on my bottles of happy pills, the ones warning me not to mix my medication with alcohol, obviously doesn't have a clue what she's talking about. While Stan dumped the old ice into the stainless steel sink under the bar and poured another double shot over some fresh cubes, I popped another pill.

"Did you get to see your family while you were back there?" Stan asked when he delivered my drink.

"Sure," I said, pouring 7-Up on top of whiskey and poking the ice. It was a lie. I called my mother once and said I'd stop by if I got time, but never did, and I didn't even take the time to phone any of my three brothers.

"That's good," Stan said, polishing the bar.

"Yeah." I was the black sheep of the family. Literally. The other Stanton boys were fair-haired with blue eyes like my father. I had dark hair, skin, and eyes. My mother is blonde Italian and always told me that I inherited the recessive Sicilian gene from her side of the family. Hell, I didn't know Sicilians had recessive genes. When I was young, my brothers teased me and said I was adopted. They turned out to be big and athletic, playing football and basketball in high school. My two older brothers, Michael and Edward, played football at Harvard on partial scholarships, stayed for law school and were now at the Washington D.C law firm our father built. James, my younger brother, switched to lacrosse in college and was now at John Hopkins doing cancer research. My high school grades weren't good enough for an Ivy League school and the only reason I got into the Coast Guard Academy was that my father called in a few favors. I bucked the Academy system the whole way and wound up on the rowing team when it turned out to be an easy way to work off some of my demerits. I was definitely the black sheep of the family.

"That scar still bothering you?" Stan asked when he noticed me scratching it.

"Must be the fog," I said. "It's driving me nuts tonight."

Everybody looked up from their drinks when Reverend Johnny came into the bar. Johnny was still wearing his old Army fatigues, but now had some fingerless wool gloves on his hands and the coffee can tucked into his left armpit. He seemed to have trouble deciding which stool he wanted, but when he finally sat down, he dumped the contents of the coffee can onto the bar. My two bucks spilled out with the rest of it.

Stan looked nervous. Beverley would have bounced Johnny's butt out of the bar and then fired Stan if she were around. But she wasn't. Stan helped Johnny count his money and then ducked under the bar to place the dinner order.

When he returned from the kitchen, Stan came down to my end of the bar looking for some sympathy. I could see in his eyes that he was afraid Beverley would return from Catalina unannounced for no other reason than to make sure Reverend Johnny stayed on the sidewalk outside.

"It looks like Reverend Johnny's back in town," I said, stating the obvious.

"Yeah," Stan said. "He was gone for awhile, but I've seen him pushing his shopping cart around town for the last few days."

I studied my drink, watching the amber whiskey currents glide around the ice cubes and mingle with the clear 7-Up, tiny bubbles rose through the drink and burst at the surface. "I wonder where he goes?"

Stan shrugged. "Who knows," he said. "I think the city gives them bus passes so they can make it to the homeless shelters when they want to." Stan paused for a moment and then added, "I know the police will give them a ride to Long Beach and dump them off if they get to bothering the locals too much on this side of the bridge."

Juanita, the plump evening cook, brought my sandwich platter from the kitchen. Reverend Johnny eyed my food as it went past him.

"Gracias," I said to Juanita.

"De nada."

My stomach growled, wanting food, but Reverend Johnny held my gaze. He wasn't looking at my food anymore. He was looking at me.

"Jesus died for your sins, too," Johnny said. "He died for all our sins."

Johnny continued to stare at me but I turned to Stan. "Jesus wasted his time on me."

"Damn it," Stan said, scurrying down to the other end of the bar to confront Johnny. "If you don't stop bothering the customers I'm going to call the cops and have them haul your ass to jail."

Reverend Johnny was a classic case of post-traumatic stress disorder if I ever saw one. A lot of guys come back from war like that. They used to call the syndrome 'shell-shocked'. After Elisha's death, I was diagnosed with everything from simple anxiety to depression to post-traumatic stress disorder. I'm not sure the doctors know what they're talking about, but now I have to see the shrink once a week to talk about my dreams and so he can make sure I'm not on the verge of suicide or some sort of violent homicidal reaction.

I ate two French fries and then took a bite of prime rib sandwich that melted in my mouth. I looked up and all the pink eyes at the bar were looking in my direction. As I took my second bite, Rachel Terazzo sat on the barstool next to mine.

"Hey," I said between chews.

"Hey."

"What's up?"

"Let's take a ride," she said, poking a straw into my drink and stealing a sip.

"I just got my food."

"Bring it with you," she said. "The shit just hit the fan."

4

In twenty-twenty hindsight, I probably should have taken my own car, but then I wouldn't have been able to eat my sandwich or find out what Rachel had going on. She wouldn't tell me anything in the bar other than that she wanted my opinion on something. Men are easy when women want their opinions. It should be considered a violation of a man's civil rights when a beautiful woman seeks his opinion.

"We sent a car over to contact Mrs. Wierman about her husband's death," Rachel said. "The Department always sends a grief counselor or psychologist out with the uniforms when they have bad news for a family."

My sandwich was dripping and I struggled to contain the pesky meat juices with napkins Stan had given me from behind the bar. Rachel looked at me when she talked, which made me nervous because the fog was pretty thick as we turned off Harbor Boulevard and headed up 25th Street. The

San Pedro Police dispatcher kept squawking on
the under dash speaker so Rachel turned it off.

"When they got to Wierman's place, they
found his wife tied up in her bathroom and the
house had been robbed," she said, looking at me
again while she talked.

"Watch where you're going," I said, clutching
my sandwich in my left hand and pointing at the
fog-bound street with my right index finger.

"Don't tell me how to drive."

"Then watch where you're going."

"I am."

"You're not looking where you're going when
you're looking at me."

"Do you want to hear this or not?"

"Yes, but watch where you're going."

Rachel had the steering wheel in a two-hand
death grip and navigated the gloomy streets of
San Pedro without talking. I was wolfing the last
of my sandwich down when I suddenly figured out
why she wanted me to come with her. Rachel
obviously didn't think what happened to Mrs.
Wierman was a coincidence.

"Are we headed to the Wierman's house?"

Rachel nodded.

"And you want me to take a look around and
tell you whether or not I think the Agency or the
Bureau has something to do with the burglary?"

She clutched the wheel tighter and nodded
again.

"I'm sorry if I hurt your feelings," I said,
bunching the dirty napkins into a ball. "But it
makes me nervous when you're not looking where
you're going."

"I know where I'm going and you didn't hurt my feelings," she said in a spousal tone reminiscent of Elisha's. "You pissed me off."

"Sorry," I said, not really meaning it, clutching the napkin ball in both hands.

"Yeah, I can tell."

The dreams about Elisha aren't as bad as they used to be. Sometimes I try talking to her instead of actually killing her, but those dreams are frustrating because I don't have a convincing argument and they go nowhere. Last night I was able to wake myself up before things got too bad. My therapist taught me that little trick, although I'm not sure how effective the technique is because then I'm awake in the middle of the night and afraid to go back to sleep. I'd been living on three to four hours of sleep for months and I was taking its toll on me.

After another five minutes of silence, Rachel turned off Paseo del Mar and onto fog-shrouded Vista Circle where the Wierman's lived and I was glad to finally get my mind off the nightmare about Elisha. Several squad cars were parked in the cul-de-sac in front of a moderate Spanish style house with white stucco exterior and a red clay tiled roof. The neighborhood had been modest middle class at one time, built in the days when San Pedro had adequate blue-collar shipyard and defense contractor jobs that paid enough for young couples to raise a family, but with today's runaway real estate market in Southern California and the burgeoning population, the Wierman's house had to worth well over a million bucks.

Rachel parked behind one of the patrol units and walked up to the house without waiting for me to get out of the car or even looking back to see if I was coming at all.

The Wierman's front lawn was manicured like a golf course putting green and the sidewalk to the front door was lined with lovingly tended beds of white begonias and red flowering ice plant. Shaped rose bushes were planted beneath the windows in front of the house, and along the used-brick lined driveway to the left, beds of mixed annuals were in full bloom. Somebody spent a lot of time gardening.

The front door was ajar so I stepped inside and closed it to about the same angle I found it. The entryway underfoot was Mexican tile and off to the left was a cozy living room where Lieutenant Richards was talking to a woman. Judging by her age and the fact that she was an emotional wreck, it had to be Mrs. Wierman. The distressed woman was sitting on a large burgundy leather sofa with her face in her hands, Lieutenant Richards sat in a chair that looked like it came from the adjacent formal dining room. He was leaning forward, talking to Mrs. Wierman in hushed tones; his usual expression had softened considerably.

Plush white carpet was the common theme throughout the house and was offset by the tiled entry that extended down a short hallway into the spacious oak floored ranch-style kitchen area where Rachel was talking to one of the uniformed officers. A white, glazed-tile table with four matching chairs sat in the corner near a large window with vertical blinds. Two full place settings and assorted condiments were still on the table. Condensation dribbled down the outside of two large crystal tumblers of water that were now devoid of ice. James Wierman would never be home for dinner again.

"Hey," I said, drawing next to Rachel.

She flashed me her 'screw you' look.

I'd seen that same look a time or two in my life, but luckily I was spared from the moment by the commotion at the front door. A woman, appearing to be in her mid-forties with layered highlighted hair, creamed-colored leather jacket, designer jeans, and high-heeled boots, burst through the door wearing a lot of jewelry and way too much perfume. She called Mrs. Wierman, *mom,* so it was easy to figure out who she was.

Lieutenant Richards left the mother and daughter alone in the living room and approached me in the kitchen. That old familiar scowl was back on his face.

I held up both hands and said, "I'm not here to step on anybody's toes or get in the way."

Lieutenant Richards looked at me for a moment before a smile cracked the corner of his mouth. It quickly turned to a smirk that said, "Gotcha."

He offered to shake hands. I accepted.

"I had Detective Terazzo bring you here," he said.

Okay, now I was confused. Especially since he had been acting so territorial aboard the *Balboa Victory* with the Federal boys. I didn't know what to say so I went with my patented non-committal smile and polite nod.

"Let's talk," he said, taking my elbow and guiding me into the white-carpeted hallway across from the living room.

The first room to the right in the hallway was set up as a typical home office. It had dark oak flooring and an oriental rug in the middle of the room. There was a set of bookshelves along the near wall, two file cabinets next to each other, and an office-sized desk under the window. All the furniture was made of stained oak. Framed photographs adorned the white stucco walls and a smaller desk in the corner opposite the window held a laptop computer and printer.

"Did Rachel fill you in on what happened."

"Somewhat."

"You don't mind helping, do you?"

"I'm not sure what I can do, you seem to pretty much have it covered."

Lieutenant Richards considered his words for a moment. "I'm just a street cop," he said. "I understand punks selling drugs, dope addicts, drunks, and men beating the shit out of their wives. But when it comes down to spies skulking around abandoned ships, well, I gotta' tell you, I'm way out of my league."

I went with the non-committal smile and polite nod again.

"Look, you've worked undercover with these guys before. You know how they think. I'm just a local street cop that's on the outside looking in."

"I'm really not sure if I can help you."

Lieutenant Richards looked at the scar on my jaw. "You really helped us out with that one. You're a fucking hero, you got to the bottom of that smuggling ring when nobody else could. I know you're connected and always have inside information about what's going down on the docks. We need your help again."

I'd been lucky with the smuggling ring bust in more ways than one. Lucky when somebody walked into my office and told me who was behind it, and even luckier when I'd gone to Mexico after the guy that tried to cut my throat.

"You get shit done. You get results."

Richards was talking about Mexico. I had been way outside of my jurisdiction, not a smart move in the first place, and I was damn lucky I didn't get fired because the State Department had to extract me and one of my Sea Marshals from a Mexican prison when the whole unsanctioned operation accumulated a body count.

"I've got a murder case and a home invasion on my hands and I'm figuring the two are connected. The CIA either killed James Wierman or they have a pretty fucking good idea who did it. I don't know what Wierman had or what he knew, but I'm guessing whoever killed him didn't get what they wanted so they came here looking for it. I've seen hundreds of home invasions and I'll tell you this, they never treat the victims as nice as they treated Mrs. Wierman, which leads me to believe it was the CIA that shook the place down."

I really didn't want to get involved in this one. It was sad the old guy was dead, but with the Bureau and the Agency already involved, there was way more going on than I wanted to know about.

"They tied her up with handkerchiefs and kept her in the bathroom for God's sake," Lieutenant Richards said. "We never see that, they always use duct tape or zip-ties and then they beat the shit out of the victims until they get what they want. That's how it goes down."

I just looked at him and blinked.

"Before I came over here tonight, I called the Bureau to find out what the hell they were doing on one of our cases and they told me they had an ongoing investigation into the accidental death of a security guard aboard the *Balboa Victory* while it was still up in Suisun Bay."

"Somebody else got killed on the *Balboa Victory*?" I asked.

"That's right. About two months ago. It could have been an accident, a weekend security guard was found at the bottom of a ladder in one of the cargo holds. The cause of death was blunt force trauma to the head, but the coroner couldn't tell if it was caused by the fall or if he was hit in the head first and then thrown down the ladder."

"What was he doing down in the cargo hold? Those guys usually hang around up on deck."

"Nobody knows, but the lay-up fleet superintendent had been getting reports of lights and noises coming from that ship so they were on alert. The FBI is checking into the possibility that looters were scrounging around on some of the ships."

"That old guy that found Wierman's body was babbling something about the ship being haunted because three sailors were killed in the cargo hold during a typhoon."

"I heard what he said, but I don't do ghosts."

"Maybe there's more to that incident than we know about."

"Hell, that was over thirty-five years ago. I can't imagine that the CIA is still worrying about three dumbass merchant seamen getting killed during the Vietnam War."

"Well, there seems to be something about that ship that keeps getting people killed."

Lieutenant Richards stepped closer and tried to look sincere. "That's why I need your help. I'm a street cop, I don't know diddly-squat about ships."

"What exactly do you want me to do?"

"I need to find out who this James Wierman was and why somebody wanted him dead. He was in the Merchant Marine, a ship's engineer from what I understand, so your agency has his service records. Maybe you could check him out from that angle."

"I could do that for you."

"And the Coast Guard is part of the Department of Homeland Security, maybe you have some contacts that could let us know if James Wierman had any sort of relationship with the CIA."

"That's harder to do," I said. "The CIA doesn't like to share information. They're funny that way."

Rachel came into the office. "Lieutenant," she said. "We need to see you."

"I'll be right there," he said to her and then turned back to me. "Take a look around the house...see if anything jumps out at you, get a feel for who this guy was and maybe we can figure out why somebody wanted him dead."

I stifled a yawn. My day began in Washington D.C. at two o'clock this morning, East Coast time, because a nightmare woke me up and I'd stayed awake to prepare my budget presentation for the congressional sub-committee. Now I was beginning a murder investigation in San Pedro. I'd been awake for almost twenty-four straight hours so far. I covered another yawn with the back of my hand as I walked over to look at the computer desk. If the CIA broke into Wierman's house looking for information, the computer would be gone. But it wasn't. I scrutinized the framed photographs on the walls. Most looked like they were candid shots of Mr. and Mrs. Wierman with their children and grandchildren. There were a few framed prints of ships; probably ships Wierman had served on. James Wierman's original Coast Guard issued Chief Engineer's license, yellowed with age, was posted on the wall under glass. I stepped closer to inspect it. The license was issued on the 7th of July 1969 in the port of San Diego.

Rachel came back into the office, stood just inside the door and looked at the floor.

"I want to apologize for snapping," she said. "I've had to put up with a lot of shit lately, and well, I'm tired."

I've been around women long enough to know that when they apologize, that's your clue to jump right in and apologize as well.

"It's my fault," I said. "I've had a long day and a really bad week."

It wasn't much of an apology, but apparently it was enough, because she stepped closer and opened her notebook.

"Here's what we have so far," she said, reading from the chicken scratches she called her notes. "Three guys in ski masks and gloves came in through the sliding glass door from the backyard. Mrs. Wierman was in the kitchen and didn't see or hear anything before they grabbed her. It happened about nine o'clock, about the same time we were on the *Balboa Victory,* and they stayed until just a couple of minutes before the patrolman and grief counselor knocked on the door."

"So they either had really good timing or a lookout."

"Right. And they took their time."

"They tied her up and kept her in her bathroom," Rachel said. "They didn't make much noise or do any talking."

"What's missing?"

"Hard to say. Mrs. Wierman is pretty freaked out right now so she's not much help. Some of her jewelry and a VCR from the bedroom are the only things she's missing so far."

"So they were here for an hour or so and that's all they took?"

"She's not really sure what else is gone, like I said, she's pretty freaked out right now."

"Sounds to me like they were looking for something specific and then just took a few things to make it look like an ordinary burglary. It shouldn't take but ten or fifteen minutes to clean out a place like this. Unless there's a safe they were trying to get into."

"No safe."

Rachel and I spent the next twenty minutes snooping through the rest of the house. The room next to the office was set up as Mrs. Wierman's sewing room. Down the hall were two larger bedrooms with full baths, one was obviously a guest room and the other was where the Wierman's slept. The odd thing was nothing was out of place. Typical thieves would have torn the place apart, dumping contents of drawers on the floor, emptying closets. And there weren't any dirty footprints on the white carpet. Neat and polite burglars. No wonder Lieutenant Richards thought the CIA was behind it.

The garage was as well organized as the rest of the house with a lavish workbench and an extensive tool assortment systematically arranged on boards and ready to use. Each tool had been outlined on the board with a red marker to indicate its proper location. Mrs. Wierman's gray Toyota was still in the garage, her husband's white Chevy Malibu was absent. Rachel said its description had been broadcast to all patrol units.

Brooke Wierman was in the kitchen getting her mother a glass of water when we came out of the garage. Rachel introduced me and I extended my condolences as I presented Brooke with a business card just like the one I'd given to the cigar smoking stranger back at the *Balboa Victory*. Brooke Wierman was as unsettled as her mother, her makeup smeared and streaked on her face.

"I'll take you back to get your car in a few minutes," Rachel said when she caught me looking at my watch.

While Rachel went to talk to her boss, I ducked into the home office again for one more look. I took the room in again. Something about it just wasn't right. And then it hit me. I didn't notice it at first, not until I'd been through the entire house and observed how orderly everything was kept. A place for everything and everything in its place. Something was missing from the office. There was a gap between pictures on the wall right next to Wierman's original Chief Engineer's license. I inspected the wall and sure enough, found a tiny nail hole. Somebody had taken one of the framed pictures and then carefully extracted the wall hanger. Judging by the size of the hole in the wall and the order of the other pictures, my guess was that a framed eight-by-ten inch photograph was missing.

"Ready?" Rachel asked when she found me.

"Yeah," I said, lingering for a moment. Given the order of the other pictures, I guessed the missing picture was either a ship or a candid shot of James Wierman with some Merchant Marine friends.

"What is it?" Rachel asked, following my eyes to the wall.

"Nothing," I said. "Just looking around."

As Rachel and I walked out of James Wierman's office, I rubbed the scar on my jaw and the itch told me that I was on the verge of getting in way over my head.

5

Rachel dropped me off at my car and I waited until she disappeared into the fog before I cut across the street to head back to the Harbor Light for a nightcap. Reverend Johnny had apparently taken his act on the road or was curled up in some alley for the night because he was nowhere to be seen. The restaurant was closed but the bar was still open and since there weren't any other customers, I got the corner seat again. Stan was restocking the beer cooler in preparation for closing and I could see in his face that he hoped I wouldn't stay, but I laid a twenty on the bar so he fetched up my usual and served it with an obligatory smile.

"Late night," noted Stan.

"Chasing bad guys."

"Catch any?"

"Nah, we only get the dumb ones. I've got a feeling these bad guys are very, very smart."

"Makes for late nights."

"You got that right."

Stan excused himself so he could continue his closing-up routine. I poked at my ice cubes and wondered why Lieutenant Richards was blowing so much smoke up my ass. I wasn't buying his poor street cop routine. He'd been around the block more times than the ice cream man and wasn't about to take any grief from the Federal boys. Sure, I could be of some help tracking down James Wierman's Merchant Marine service record and maybe, just maybe, it might have something to do his present predicament. I guess you could call being dead a predicament. The only reason I could figure that Lieutenant Richards wanted me involved was that he was making sure he had a back door. That way he could push as hard as he wanted and if things got too heavy with the CIA, he could save face by turning the investigation over to me and calling it a Homeland Security problem. Just slip out the old back door. But then again, maybe he had something else up his sleeve.

When she gave me a ride back to my car, Rachel told me that the snuff film case was coming to trial within the month. She'd been working with the District Attorney and things weren't going entirely ducky for her. New photographs of her had surfaced and the defense was planning on doing everything to discredit her testimony. I'd seen the earlier tabloid pictures of her dressed up as a dominatrix and she didn't look bad. Black leather suited her. I know the good old boys at the police department have been giving her a lot of, "I've been a bad boy and I need to be spanked." Now I kind of felt bad that I'd pissed her off.

The feeling of impending doom was creeping into my stomach so I washed another pill down with the last of my drink. I checked the date of the prescription on the bottle and did a quick inventory of how many pills I had left. I was taking a lot of pills. Too many lately. Good thing I had more than one doctor writing me prescriptions. At least I'm not an addict. Addicts tell themselves they can quit anytime, but I have my feet planted firmly in reality. There's no way I can quit the pills.

Stan tried not to look perturbed when I tapped my glass on the bar to indicate I was dry. He forced another smile when he brought me the drink. I slid the twenty across the bar and said he could keep the change and close the register because I was headed home in a few minutes. Timing is everything when mixing medication with alcohol. I needed sleep some kind of bad, and right now, my blood chemistry was getting close to where it needed to be.

When I started to nod out at the bar, I slugged the rest of my drink down and said goodnight to Stan. I tottered a bit when I left my barstool, wavering as I tried to find the handle to the front door, but the chilly midnight mist brought me around a little. Considering the condition I was in, I was glad I didn't have to make the thirty-five minute suicide drive to Huntington Beach anymore. The house I'd been renting for the last couple of years had finally sold, and once clear of the lease, I'd found a place closer to the office.

My legs felt like they weighed a ton as I walked to my car and it was almost as if I were on autopilot as I drove through the fog up 4th Street toward Gaffey. I lingered at the stop sign and when I was sure no traffic was coming out of the fog, I took a quick left, driving up Gaffey to 17th where I went right and climbed to the top of San Pedro Hill. It took a moment for me to realize the black wrought iron gate in front of me was the entrance to the underground parking of the Bonita Apartments where I lived. I fumbled with the battery powered opener I kept stashed above my sun visor and the gate slid open, the electric motor groaning as it struggled to move the massive security gate on its rollers.

There was a red Jeep Wrangler with a white bimini top parked askew in one of my two assigned parking spaces. I hadn't seen it before but figured it probably belonged to a girlfriend of one of the Reynoza brothers that lived down the hall from me on the third floor of the five-story apartment building. The Reynoza brothers changed girlfriends as often as they changed their underwear. Maybe more often.

I didn't feel like fooling with my suitcase but knew I'd need my toiletries and a clean uniform in the morning so I muled it out of the trunk and over to the elevator. After I punched the 'up' button three times, I rested my forehead against the cool metal door and waited for the elevator. When the doors opened, I woke up, wheeled my suitcase inside and punched the third floor button three times. I could hear the Reynoza brothers' party even before the elevator doors opened.

Julio and Ernesto Reynoza moved into the building about two months ago. Actually, it was more like they crash landed. They threw a party the first night and it has been going on ever since. The Reynoza brothers were longshoremen, working different shifts, and their two-bedroom apartment would put most sports bars to shame. They have it set up with four large-screen televisions hooked to a satellite link that plays sports from around the world night and day. There's a constant stream of longshore buddies, girls, and booze coming into the apartment. They must need a skip-loader to empty their trash every morning. The cops have been summoned so many times that they don't even bother to show up anymore, but instead, call on the phone and ask the brothers to try and hold it down a little. It turns out that their mother is on the staff of the four-term city councilman from the harbor district and that's one tree no local cop is going to shake if he cares about his job.

"You're back, Jared," said a barefoot Julio Reynoza that was naked except for a baggy pair of blue and white striped boxers. He was standing in his open doorway with one hand on the waist of some cute little blonde and a bottle of beer in the other. His eyes were as glassy as mine felt. "Want a beer?"

"Nah, sleep. But thanks."

"Come on, just one."

"Yeah," cooed the blonde. "You're cute, join the party."

"Next time," I said as I dragged my suitcase down the hallway three more doors. I'm glad I didn't live next door to them. Three doors down on the same floor was bad enough.

Since I don't have pets or plants, the sparsely furnished two-bedroom apartment was just like I'd left it last week. Other than the answering machine that is. It was beeping incessantly and the red light was flashing but I wasn't going to deal with the answering machine now. It could wait until later. I turned my cell phone off and plugged it into the charger in the kitchen, made a quick bathroom stop, closed the bedroom door so I wouldn't hear the answering machine, and was between the sheets before my blood chemistry could change.

Fortunately, I got a pretty good night's sleep. There was a commotion in the hall just after three o'clock that woke me up. It sounded like a fight, but was probably just the Reynoza brother's party spilling out of their apartment. I was able to go back to sleep, avoiding dreams about Elisha. The phone rang at a quarter past five and interrupted the disjointed dream I was having about my father. A hundred more hours of sleep would have been nice, but since that wasn't likely, I forced myself to get out of bed and dug a set of gray Coast Guard sweats from the top drawer of the dresser. I hadn't worked out in a week and really needed it now.

While the coffee was brewing, I surveyed the inside of the refrigerator to see what there was to eat. Curdled milk, ten-day-old Chinese or twelve-day-old Mexican leftovers, and some vegetables in plastic bags turning to liquid. The damn fridge was scarier than usual. I scrounged two eggs to go with a freezer-burned English muffin and started breakfast while I listened to my phone messages. There was the usual rash of telemarketers and a call from my mother. The last call, the one at a quarter past five this morning, was a hang-up but I figured it was just a wrong number or the Reynozas asking me to join the party.

I munched the English muffin slathered with peanut butter that was on the verge of going stale, sipped hot black coffee, and tried to recall the details of the dream about my father. I'd have to talk about the dream on Friday with my shrink. I was supposed to keep a log of my dreams and as many details as I could remember. For some reason my dream log was pretty sketchy.

My father passed away a little over a year ago, eight months after Elisha died. In the dream he wasn't ill yet, he was sitting behind the massive cherry desk in his study, looking over his glasses at me. I took a sip of coffee and could almost hear him say, "Young man..." A shiver went up my spine just thinking about all the ass-chewings I got when I was young.

The study was my father's center of power. Countless late night meetings with senior members of congressional staffs took place there, political deals made, careers planned or ruined. The course of the nation being shaped. Quid pro quo.

Maybe I had the dream because I'd driven by our old Tappahannock, Virginia house last week.

I sat in my car across the street from the white-pillared plantation style residence for an hour, half expecting boys to come outside to play football on the front lawn like my brothers used to do. It didn't happen.

An oil painting of Robert E. Lee hung on the wall behind my father's desk. Supposedly, it was a Civil War era original given to my father by a senator from Georgia. I'm not sure what happened to it after my father died, but I can still picture the look in the Confederate General's blue eyes. In my teens, I would spend hours in front of a mirror trying to get that same look in my eyes.

After I put my plate in the sink with last week's dirty dishes, I began my workout. I stretched on the living room carpet for five minutes, did fifty sit-ups, fifty push-ups, then moved to the spare bedroom where I had my weight bench set up and went through my routine, concentrating on repetitions more than weight. When I began to sweat, I was ready to row.

The clean uniform in my suitcase was still encased in a plastic Marriott hotel bag. I packed it as well as everything else I'd need to get ready for work in a black duffel and locked my apartment door as I left. The televisions were still blaring as I passed the Reynoza brothers' apartment but I didn't hear any voices. The red Jeep was gone from my parking spot.

The iron security gate rolled back to reveal the leaden morning sky. The fog had thinned to a translucent veil after sunrise, but the night mist left behind a dewy film as shiny as fresh varnish that coated the streets and cars of San Pedro. I pulled into the mini-mart at Eighth and Pacific, finding it busier than usual for six o'clock in the morning, and had to wait in line to get my morning Red Bull. The Bull chased the first pill of the day and I listened to the news on the car radio while I drove along Harbor Boulevard. This time of day it was only a ten-minute drive to the San Pedro Fire Department's boathouse at Berth 194. I leaned out the window and swiped my access card at the security box and when the chain link security gate rolled back far enough, I pulled through and parked into a designated visitor's parking spot.

The finely crafted wooden scull was built by the same shop that built the eight-man boats for the Dartmouth rowing team and was a graduation present from my father. The San Pedro Fire Department allowed me keep it in the boathouse with their two massive and immaculately maintained fireboats. Rank has its privileges. I pulled the blue flannel cover from the hull and quickly inspected it for damage before hoisting it above my head. I took the boat out to the pontoon dock that jutted into the harbor's east basin and went back for the oars.

Visibility was about a quarter mile in the ship channel and I briefly considered rowing to work like I often did. There wasn't room in the boat for my duffel so I'd have to plan ahead and do it another time. Maybe tomorrow.

The gray sweats weren't much of a barrier against the early morning chill. I had cooled down and stiffened up since my workout, so when I started rowing, I took it easy. I rowed east in the Cerritos Channel toward Westside Marina, concentrating on my breathing and the formation of each fluid stroke of the oars; the water murmuring by the veneer hull was an intoxicating whisper.

Elisha loved it when I took her rowing. She would lie in the bow of my grandfather's old white dory, reading a book and soaking up the sun, while I worked up river to find a secluded picnic spot. Her memory brought tightness to my chest so I tried to empty my mind while concentrating on my form.

The Cerritos Channel railroad and highway bridges passed overhead, tires of cars and trucks thumping rhythmically over the gaps in the drawbridge. As I approached the marina, I passed the tug *Sea Hawk* on her way to a morning job assignment. The tug captain recognized me and waved. I had my hands full of oars so I just nodded. The almost imperceptible wake of the tug threatened to swamp my fragile craft and I adjusted my course to quarter the waves.

Once past the *Sea Hawk*, I executed a 180-degree turn and began a sprint back down the waterway. I shot past the work-bound tugboat like she was standing still and the captain grinned as he honored me with a short blast on the tug's whistle, the baritone signal resonating off the ships lining the main shipping channel. I continued my sprint all the way down to the Vincent Thomas Bridge and the main turning basin where I made a sweeping right turn and rowed at a more leisurely pace back toward the boathouse. The *Sea Hawk* was passing a hawser up to a massive oil tanker at Berth 172 as I passed her once again.

I was on my knees and pulling the scull onto the pontoon dock when Rachel Terazzo said, "I figured I'd find you here."

"What's up?"

"Want to get some coffee?"

I stood up and hoisted the boat over my head. "I've got to go to work."

"I won't stop you."

"You look tired." I said to her.

"Two more homicides last night."

"Anything interesting?"

"Nope. Just a bunch of gangbangers shooting at each other up in Wilmington.

I edged the scull past her on the pontoon dock and headed for the boathouse.

"I want to take a look at the *Balboa Victory* in the daylight," she said, following me. "There isn't anybody around until after eight. We could have breakfast, take a quick look around, talk to a few people, and then you could be to work by nine."

"Why are you so interested in this?"

"I don't know. Guess I feel bad for the old guy and his wife. Somebody fucked his family over and they should pay for it."

I continued walking toward the boathouse. "What time is it now?"

"Seven-twenty."

After I put the boat back on its rack, I retrieved the oars, setting one on each side of the hull, then spread the blue flannel cover over the whole rig.

"What do you say? I'll buy if you go back to the ship with me."

"What are you hoping to find?"

"I'm not sure," she said, fingering the firearm on her hip with her left hand. "But not finding anything may tell us as much as finding something."

She had a point. If the CIA were involved, there wouldn't be much left behind to find. Just the thought of digging around the same cesspool as the CIA would normally make me wary. Unfortunately, my medication had kicked in and my give-a-shit factor was low.

"I have to shower."

"No you don't, not to walk around a rusty mothballed ship."

Rachel had her windbreaker tucked behind her Colt Python, exposing it, and her face was painted with that strung out and tired look of somebody coming down from an adrenalin rush. Police work is usually long periods of boredom interrupted by moments of sheer terror. I could only imagine working a couple of gangbanger homicides. No telling when the shooting would start again.

"I need to change clothes," I said, scratching the scar on my jaw.

"So change."

There was a noon luncheon I had to attend and all the paperwork still on my desk, but other than that, there wasn't a good reason not to go to get a cup of coffee with Rachel. Something told me there was more on Rachel's mind than looking around the *Balboa Victory* in the daylight; she'd never tracked me down at the boathouse before.

Rachel half-heartedly batted her eyelashes at me, a technique I'm sure usually works quite well for her, but this morning her eyes lacked the sultry sparkle they had last night when she got me to leave the Harbor Light with her. I wasn't sure what was bothering her, but there was only one way to find out.

6

Rachel wanted to go to the Mayan Café, which was a Mexican restaurant, but she ordered the French toast. The rowing session made me hungry so I went with Wednesday's breakfast special, a Huevos Rancheros platter, and was trying not to dribble it down the front of my last clean uniform.

"Any leads on the Wierman case yet?" I asked, making small talk. Rachel was forking at her French toast, more mutilating it than eating it.

"A patrol unit found his car at a mini-mall over in Lomita a few hours ago," Rachel said. "It was parked in front of a dry cleaners."

"Did you find anything interesting in it?"

"I haven't looked at it yet, I was busy on another homicide. They're towing the car in and the crime lab will go over it."

Rachel stabbed a piece of French toast, absently holding it aloft on her fork while she rested her elbows on the table. Her eyes reflected that she'd drifted somewhere else.

"How about Mrs. Wierman?"

Rachel blinked and looked at me, setting the fork and French toast back on her plate. "What about her?" She sat forward in her chair, elbows still on the table.

"How's she doing?"

The waitress walked by and topped off our coffees. Rachel added another creamer and pack of sugar to hers.

"Mrs. Wierman is a wreck," she said, pausing to down some coffee. "She did say that her husband came home mad as hell about a week ago."

"Mad? Not scared?"

"No, she said mad."

"About what?"

"She didn't know. She said he was originally excited about taking the job as Chief Engineer on the *Balboa Victory* because they were going to dry-dock the ship and do a lot of work to it in the next few weeks. But then he went to a meeting, and when he came home, he was furious."

"He didn't tell her what he was mad about?"

"She said she leaves him alone when he gets like that. Her secret to keeping a good marriage or some such bullshit." Rachel had her elbows on the table, holding her coffee cup in two hands. "That's why I wanted to take a look at the ship in the daylight. Maybe we can figure out why he was so mad."

I knew I'd be sorry later if I finished the Huevos Rancheros platter with all the beans and salsa, so I pushed it away, keeping the remains of a flour tortilla to go with my coffee. Besides, my uniform was still clean and considering my luck lately, I didn't need to tempt fate.

Rachel had checked out again, still holding the coffee cup to her face with two hands. She looked tired. Dog-tired. She'd been up all night. But I also knew the kind of fatigue I saw in her face was just a symptom. It's the kind of fatigue that goes clean to the bone and behind it there was something deeper, more complex going on. That manic thousand-mile look in the eyes always gives it away. It was a look I'd seen before. In my own bathroom mirror.

"Are you okay?"

She looked at her coffee cup and then set it on the table. "Sure. Why?"

"Just checking," I said, trying my best noncommittal smile. "Do you want to talk about it?"

The rage welled up in her eyes and I knew it was just the tip of the iceberg. Her lips trembled. She was trying to hold something huge inside.

"What to you want to hear? All the details? You're a pervert like all the rest!" She knocked over her water glass as she got up from the table and stormed out the front door.

I dropped a twenty on the table for the waitress, hoping it would be enough for breakfast and the tip, and then followed Rachel into the parking lot where she was sitting on the hood of her car refusing to cry. She wouldn't look at me so I took a place near her, leaning my butt against her car.

How do you even begin to tell somebody that you understand what they're going through and they aren't alone? Especially when you can't even deal with it yourself.

It's the undercover work that does it to you. Oh sure, it's fun at first; it's like dressing up for a costume party. You get to pretend to be somebody else. It's easy, and at the end of the day, you just take your costume off and go home. But you don't fall down with a short hard blow, you shuffle along until you lose your load of the moral code and you can't tell right from wrong. You try the coke, let somebody take pictures of you in leather, have illicit sex with somebody you shouldn't, all the while telling yourself it's just part of the job and it's okay because it's not really who you are. Eventually you can't separate your two lives, you never leave that undercover person behind and he's always inside you whispering in your ear, "You liked that, didn't you?" and you try not to admit the truth to yourself because the truth is that you really did like it and it was wrong.

It took about five minutes for Rachel to lock away her demons and pull herself together enough to look at me. I could see she was having trouble finding something appropriate to say so I cut her some slack and said, "Do you want to look at that ship now?"

She nodded and slipped off the hood of her car.

"I wish I could tell you it gets easier," I said, holding up the bottle of pills from my pocket. I shook the plastic bottle and the contents inside sounded like a rattlesnake just before it strikes.

"I'll let you know if I ever get to the point I can stop taking these."

Rachel pulled into the lot at Berth 94 and parked in front of the Merchant Marine Veteran's Association office building, a modest green and white one-story modular unit that was as new as the parking lot. We'd driven separate cars so I took the space next to hers and waited for her to get out of her car, but when I looked over, I saw she was talking on her cell phone. I decided to stretch my legs while I waited.

The *Dixie Victory* was docked right behind the *Balboa Victory* and it was a classic before and after picture. The *Dixie Victory* was shipshape, Bristol fashion, and as slick as a baby's bottom. The *Balboa Victory* looked like somebody hit it with the ugly stick. Both ships displayed a red 'S' shaped seahorse on their smokestacks, indicating they were operated by a company called SeaTrans, one of the port's major shipping lines. The *Balboa Victory*'s seahorse was faded and peeling while her sistership's stack insignia was pristine.

Shortly after eight o'clock, the parking lot began to fill up. Men in work clothes filed aboard the *Balboa Victory*, a few were older, probably retired Merchant Marine Veterans, but most were young, hardly more than teenagers.

Rachel wasn't talking when she got out of her car and dug a couple of flashlights from the trunk. I wasn't about to make the mistake of asking her again if she was okay. I followed her up the *Balboa Victory*'s gangway and on deck we were stopped by a wiry old seaman dressed in denim dungarees, a light-blue chambray shirt, and a navy blue cap that had 'U.S.S. DEWEY-DD 349' embroidered in gold letters above the bill.

"I'm Bosun Browder," he said, extending a leathered hand. "Are you here to work or to sightsee?"

Rachel flashed her badge.

"Which one of these squids are you looking for?" he asked. "They're all worthless."

Just aft of the gangway, was a large stack of metal crates similar to the ones I'd seen last night in the cargo hold and a dozen or so youths were loitering nearby, joking, smoking, and generally acting immature.

Bosun Browder hadn't heard about James Wierman's murder yet and listened intently as Rachel gave her account of what had happened last night. Then Browder explained to us that the youths were all volunteers from Cabrillo Vo-Tech in Harbor City. Each one was enrolled in courses preparing them to become electricians, plumbers, welders, or painters and they were receiving credit toward graduation for 'on the job' experience they got working aboard the ship.

We told him we wanted to look around and Browder told us to help ourselves, just be careful of the roped off or chalk-marked areas where the deck was wasted and too thin to support much weight.

Bosun Browder was seventy if he was a day, but he turned on his heels, a spring in his step, and started barking orders to the Vo-Tech slave labor. I overheard a smart-ass remark about Browder being old and then heard him reply, "Me mother was a mermaid and me father was King Neptune. I was born on the crest of a wave and rocked in the cradle of the deep, seaweed and barnacles are me clothes. Every hair on me head is hemp, every bone in me body's a spar, and when I spits, I spits tar. I'se hard, I is, I am, I are."

The first place we poked around was #3 cargo hold where James Wierman's body was originally found. The portable lights were gone and we probed the darkness with the beams of our flashlights. I was curious about the metal boxes and began opening the ones that were easy to get to. Most of the boxes were stenciled 'Property of U.S. Maritime Administration' and contained assorted engine and deck department spare parts, logbooks, stationary, lifeboat rations, etc. Nothing too exciting. Rachel inspected the chalk outline of where James Wierman was found.

"Let's check out these drag marks," she said.

The drag marks were easy to follow in the cargo hold because of the grime on the deck and they led to a watertight door between the cargo hold and the engineroom machine shop. The engineroom was well illuminated and the deck of the machine shop was freshly painted a mahogany red that was going to make blood hard to spot.

"This is as far as we could follow them last night," Rachel said, examining the deck for marks with her flashlight beam. "There aren't blood pools or anything else to indicate a struggle took place here, but he was definitely dragged through this door."

"What do you know about his time of death?" I asked.

"According to his body temperature, time of death was somewhere between four and five in the afternoon."

"I wonder what he was working on?"

"Who knows?"

"Maybe he kept a maintenance log. If we could find that, we might know what he was working on yesterday afternoon."

Rachel and I meandered through the cavernous engineroom with its multi-layered catwalks and platforms, carefully watching for blood, grease smears, or signs of a project that hadn't been completed. We weren't really sure what we were looking for and nothing really caught our attention.

"I wonder if he had some of those Vo-Tech kids working for him yesterday," I said. "Maybe they would know something."

"That's a possibility. Let's look around a little more and then we'll go ask." Rachel rested on a stool at the watch engineer's log desk on the main engine throttle control flat. From the log desk the watch engineer could monitor the myriad of gauges associated with the operation of the steam turbine engine and its boilers, fuel, feedwater, and electrical systems.

I looked through the log desk but didn't find anything, not even a notepad or a pencil.

"This place is spooky," Rachel said.

There was an occasional groan, clang, or creak to break up the eerie silence in the engineroom.

In the background, somewhere far away, we heard the faint splashing sound of running water.

"Let's find that," Rachel said.

I pointed in the direction of the sound and we dropped down one more level, working our way aft in the engineroom, stopping frequently to make sure we were headed in the right direction. We were standing on the deck plate just above the bilge, shining our lights into the darkness below, when suddenly a piece of machinery not more than fifteen feet away thundered to life, the racket reverberating through the engineroom like we were inside a drum.

Rachel grabbed my arm.

"Shit!" she said. "What the hell's that?"

I walked over and shined my light on the whining electric motor that was about the size of a large microwave oven and read the nameplate next to it. "Bilge pump," I said.

The battleship-gray pump ran for about fifteen seconds and then shut itself off. The eerie silence returned to the engineroom.

"I think I know what's going on," I said as I approached a tunnel that was about a hundred-fifty feet long, five feet high, and six feet wide. Watertight light globes were spaced at about fifteen foot intervals above the two-foot diameter steel shaft that turned the ship's propeller and ran down the center of the alleyway that was located beneath #4 and #5 cargo holds. A narrow steel-plated walkway ran next to the shaft and a rusty pipe safety rail separated the walkway from the shaft that was obviously very dangerous when it was turning. I had to duck and turn sideways to move in the cramped space.

"This is the shaft alley," I informed her.

"Nice," Rachel said. "Where are we going?"

"I think I know where the water's coming from."

It took us a couple of minutes to reach the end of the shaft alley and sure enough, there was a trickle of water entering at the bottom of the shaft where it passes through the hull. At the end of the shaft alley was a vertical escape trunk and ladder that led up to the main deck of the ship.

"The stern tube is leaking, that's where the water in the bilge is coming from." I shined my light into the bilge and saw several large wrenches sitting on a plastic five-gallon bucket. "Somebody was trying to fix the leak."

"Maybe this is where Wierman was working."

"Maybe," I said, looking around the area for blood, hair, or sign of a struggle. We were a long way from where Wierman's body was found, and if somebody killed him here, it would have been a major project to get him to where he ended up.

"There's nothing here," Rachel said after a few moments. "This place is freaking me out, let's go."

On our way out of the shaft alley I noticed something I hadn't seen before because I'd been concentrating on the trickling water.

"What are you looking at?" Rachel asked.

I flashed my light around the area, illuminating flaking paint and rust, and then turned the beam on an inspection plate on the steel bulkhead next to the walkway. The oval steel plate was about three feet high and two feet wide, held in place by twenty or so large nuts on steel bolts penetrating the bulkhead.

"No rust," I said as I touched the grease on the threads of one of the bolts. "Somebody has pulled this inspection plate recently." I rapped my knuckles on the steel and it sounded hollow.

"What's on the other side?"

"My guess is that these are fuel tanks. Empty ones."

"James Wierman had grease on his clothes," Rachel said as she touched one of the bolts, rubbing the grease between her fingers. "Maybe we should take a sample."

"There's grease all over this ship and there's no telling where he got his."

We considered the grease dilemma for a few moments and then Rachel said, "Let's go, I've been up all night and need to go home so I can get some sleep."

Since it was almost nine, I concurred and we made our way back to the main deck. Bosun Browder had his deck gang hauling the metal boxes from the stack on deck down to #3 cargo hold and stowing them with the others we'd looked at earlier.

"Did you find what you wanted?" Browder asked.

"We were just looking," Rachel said.

"I have a question for you," I said to Browder.

"Shoot."

"Have you been doing any work in the engineroom?"

"Not me, but the Chief has been down there every day."

"You mean James Wierman."

"Yes, he's been here every day."

"Did he use any of the Vo-Tech volunteers?"

"I'm not really sure what he had lined up for help, but I'm guessing that he probably did use some of them from time to time. We have quite a few want-to-be welders and electricians in the group. Right now I've got them lugging these heavy-assed boxes around. At sea that's considered skilled labor."

"Do you know if he had any help yesterday afternoon?"

"Like I said, I'm not really sure what was going on in the engineroom, but I'll tell you this much. The Vo-Tech kids only work mornings, so they wouldn't have been helping him yesterday afternoon."

"Was anybody else with him yesterday afternoon?"

"I wouldn't know." Bosun Browder smiled. "There's an old expression you hear a lot on these ships."

"What's that?"

"I'd rather have three sisters in a whorehouse than a brother in the engineroom," Browder said. "The deck and engine departments on these ships don't mix, we each pretty much keep to ourselves."

"Why's that?" Rachel asked.

"Tradition," said Browder. "And on these ships, you don't fuck with tradition."

7

Since we were already parked in front of the Merchant Marine Veterans Association office, Rachel and I decided to stop in and ask a few questions. Just inside the front door was a chest-high counter strewn with brochures for tours and events aboard the *Dixie Victory*. Behind the counter in the efficient one-room office, there were six budget-minded steel desks, an assortment of filing cabinets, and a large coffee bar that was complete with several dozen doughnuts. Framed photographs showing the *Dixie Victory* at various stages of her renovation lined the walls along with several large World War Two era Merchant Marine posters. I suspected that the building was used as a forum for Veterans to tell sea stories and relive the old days more than it was used as a real office.

"Do you need tickets for one of our tours?" asked the middle-aged secretary who had the place all to herself this early in the morning. She wore a pink pantsuit, early 70's style hair lacquered in place, bright red lipstick that matched her nails, and a nametag that identified her as Corrine Stark.

"We're investigating the death of James Wierman," Rachel said, flashing her badge.

Corrine's polite smile vanished and she quickly donned an expression on her face like she'd just stepped in dog poop.

"I'm so sorry to hear about what happened to Jim," Corrine said. "But all inquiries are to be directed to Malcolm Cross."

Rachel and I looked at each other. That was fast. The Association already had damage control in place. 'Loose Lips Sink Ships' was the Merchant Marine motto in World War Two. The Veterans Association hadn't forgotten.

"When will Malcolm Cross be in?" Rachel asked.

"Oh, he doesn't work here," Corrine said. "He's over at SeaTrans headquarters."

"I have a question about the Vo-Tech volunteers," Rachel said. "Does this office keep track of what days and hours each volunteer works?"

Corrine looked nervous. "I'm sorry, but all inquiries are to be directed to Malcolm Cross."

"But Mr. Cross doesn't work here."

"That's right, he's at SeaTrans headquarters."

"So who keeps track of volunteer hours here?" snapped Rachel, showing her frustration.

Corrine's face hardened. "You'll have to talk to Malcolm Cross."

"Fine."

Outside, there was a bright silver spot low in the eastern sky where the sun was trying to penetrate the persistent marine layer. A massive, black-hulled Korea Line ship slipped down the channel behind the two old Victory ships on its way to the main turning basin, her rows of cargo containers jutting ten stories high. As the modern vessel moved up the channel, it blotted out the sky, dwarfing the smaller antique vessels in the foreground.

"What now?" I asked.

"Now I go home and get some sleep. The day shift can handle this bullshit," Rachel said. "I don't need it, I've got to work again tonight."

The main engine of the Korea Line ship rumbled to life, acrid black smoke burbling from its stack. Shrill whistles from the assist tugs signaled the commencement of the containership's turning maneuver beneath the Vincent Thomas Bridge.

Rachel paused, looking at me over the roof of her car. "Thanks," she said.

"Sure." I watched her drive away, wondering why she thanked me. Was it because I bought her breakfast or because I came with her to look at the *Balboa Victory*? I damn sure hadn't done much else. Maybe she was thanking me because I didn't do anything else to piss her off this morning.

After I started my car, I called my office to check in with Yeoman Jenkins, the lanky ex-Iowa farm boy who served as secretary for the harbor security office. He welcomed me back to town and then informed me that although there wasn't anything urgent at the moment, he said my desk could be considered a disaster area and then he reminded me that I had a noon luncheon to attend.

It was a quarter past nine now, a little more than twelve hours since Rachel first called me, and the circumstances around James Wierman's death were getting more bizarre by the moment. I did a quick inventory of the facts in my head. Wierman's house had been burglarized after he was killed, somebody went to great pains to move his body into #3 cargo hold where three other seamen had died years ago, the FBI was investigating another death aboard the same ship, The CIA tried to claim the body, and now the Veteran's Association was doing damage control under the direction of some slick-willie from SeaTrans. I was puzzled as to why somebody from SeaTrans was handling everything because Wierman's death occurred aboard a ship that belonged to the Merchant Marine Veteran's Association. What was the connection? I looked over at the SeaTrans stack insignias on the two Victory ships and decided to pay Mr. Malcolm Cross a visit in order to satisfy my curiosity.

As I made a left turn onto Harbor Boulevard from the Berth 94 parking lot, I saw Reverend Johnny working the west side of the street at the bottom of the freeway ramp. He had his shopping cart, 'Will Work For Food' sign, and was wearing headphones while trying to wave down cars.

The SeaTrans home office was located in a contemporary steel and glass twelve story commercial building in downtown San Pedro on the corner of Ninth Street and Hermosa Avenue, just two blocks up the hill from Harbor Boulevard and walking distance from the Harbor Light bar. I parked in the underground lot, took the stairs to the lobby, and approached the information desk being attended by an attractive young brunette who looked like she should still be in high school.

"Where are the SeaTrans offices?"

The brunette checked her list. "Twelfth floor," she said, pointing in the direction of the elevators.

There was nobody else on the elevator and it went straight to the twelfth floor without stopping. *Jumping Jack Flash* by the Rolling Stones accompanied me on my vertical ascent. Since when did the Rolling Stones become elevator music?

Another young brunette was behind the reception desk on the twelfth floor.

"Commander Stanton to see Malcolm Cross," I said.

"Do you have an appointment?"

"I'm with the Coast Guard and investigating a murder, I don't need an appointment."

The expression on her face informed me I was being rude. "Have a seat," she said, waving her French manicure in the direction of several large blue leather couches and chairs that formed an impromptu waiting area. "I'll see if he's available."

The view of the harbor from the waiting area was spectacular and I could see that the behemoth Korea Line containership had finished the required 180-degree turn under the bridge and was approaching her berth on the east side of the main shipping channel. I sat patiently in the waiting area, watching the activity in the busiest harbor in the nation, and just about the time I resigned myself to the fact that I was getting the run-around, I heard someone call my name.

Malcolm Cross was a couple inches shy of six feet, broad at the shoulder, with intense but friendly brown eyes and dressed in a tailored light-blue Italian suit. His hair and skin put him somewhere in his sixties while his vice-grip handshake said he was no pushover.

"We've met," he said. "At Admiral Ballard's luncheon a couple of months ago."

"Sure," I said, taking my hand back. I remembered the event that Admiral Ballard hosted but didn't remember meeting Malcolm Cross there. The luncheon took place at the Officer's Club in Alameda and Admiral Ballard, the Commandant of the Eleventh Coast Guard District, used the occasion to introduce a number of Capitol Hill bigwigs to the movers and shakers in the West Coast shipping industry. The Coast Guard has always been the bastard child of the armed services, the only one to reside outside the walls of the Pentagon, and as a result, was always on the bottom of the list when it came to military spending. The purpose of Admiral Ballard's luncheon had been an attempt to change that. The Coast Guard's early roots were with the Treasury Department where its role was to control smuggling, eventually moving to the Transportation Department with the additional responsibility to maintain navigational aids and shipping safety. More recently, the Coast Guard was shuffled to the Department of Homeland Security where harbor safety was added as a top priority to its long list of responsibilities, but money for operations is harder than ever to come by.

"What can I do for you Commander Stanton?" Malcolm Cross asked.

Most people wouldn't have even picked it up, the ever so subtle pugnacious glint in his eye, the commencement of the cat and mouse game. But I'd played this game with my father for over thirty years. Always losing of course. But I did get better over time, maybe even battling him to a few standoffs before he died.

"I was referred here by Corrine Stark," I said, glancing at my shoes, signaling submission. I'd learned this game from the master. Rule number one is to allow your opponent to underestimate you.

"Corrine Stark?" he said, feigning.

"Yes, Corrine Stark with the Merchant Marine Veterans office," I said, eagerness tainting my response, blood in the water to tempt the shark. "I had a couple of questions concerning James Wierman and she referred me here."

"Of course," Malcolm Cross said, palm upward gesturing down the hall. "Come into my office and I'll see if I can't answer your questions."

In poker they call it a 'tell', but whatever you want to call it, it was a dead giveaway that Malcolm Cross felt he had me in the palm of his hand and under control. I stayed a step behind him as we walked to the office, another sign of submission.

"How's your mother?" he asked, looking over his right shoulder.

"Fine, thanks for asking."

His question wasn't as friendly as it would seem and it spoke volumes to me. First of all, I didn't remember meeting him at Admiral Ballard's luncheon because he wasn't there. That was a bluff on his part. Secondly, while I was in the waiting room, he was making phone calls to find out exactly who I was and why I was there. Thirdly, by asking about my mother, he told me he knew about my father and that my brothers were well connected on Capitol Hill. Lastly, he had immediate access to a lot of information. He knew all about me, but I had no idea who he was. Advantage Malcolm Cross.

"Have a seat," he said, lowering himself into a generous chair behind an immense mahogany desk.

The office was as impressive as any I'd ever seen. It had floor to ceiling windows on the south side, facing the Pacific Ocean with what had to be a million dollar view of Catalina Island on a clear day. The furniture was exquisite leather and the carpet French wool. In one corner was an extensive wet bar and sitting area for more informal occasions. I'd expected to see pictures of ships in the office, but instead, there was an extraordinary collection of African game mounts adorning three walls.

"You're quite the hunter," I said.

"Not really." He motioned for me to be seated. "Golf and tennis are more to my liking."

There were two plush armchairs in front of the desk and I chose the one on the left that gave me less reflected light on his face. The chair was deeper and more comfortable than expected and I sank into it as if being pulled by a magnet.

We considered each other in silence.

"This isn't my office," he offered. "It belongs to Franklin Sheridan, the SeaTrans CEO. Maybe you've heard that he's been quite ill lately."

"I'm sorry to hear that."

Franklin Sheridan was the all-American success story. He had started a small transportation company in the early sixties as a ship owner-operator and built it into a burgeoning shipping line that saw unbridled growth at a time other American shipping companies were drowning in red ink. Somewhere along the line, he took the company public and made more money than you could shake stick at. I knew the story because Franklin Sheridan donated millions to charity and had an uncanny knack for being seen in the right places at the right times. He was famous for throwing elaborate and high profile fundraisers at his lavish Punta Bonita mansion. Now he was dying and there wasn't enough money in the world to change the inevitable. How does that nursery rhyme go? 'All the king's horses and all the king's men couldn't put Humpty-Dumpty back together again.'

"I take it that you're filling in as CEO in his absence?"

Malcolm Cross laughed and shifted in his chair. "No, not at all, the board of directors is running the company quite well. I'm the Public and Community Relations Administrator. We've outgrown the twelfth floor and office space is at a premium. My ending up with this office was just luck of the draw."

"Nice," I said, nodding approval, trying not to let on that I wasn't buying it. The Chief Executive Officer of a corporation like SeaTrans doesn't give up his office to some clown from Public Relations just because he's sick. A shipping company is made up of ship operations personnel, engineers that build ships, cargo brokers, risk management experts, a maritime lawyer or two, and the bean counters in finance that hold it all together. What the public or community thinks is of little concern to an international shipping company. Besides, even if SeaTrans did have somebody to handle public and community relations, they wouldn't be using some high-horsepowered stud in a tailored Italian suit.

"You said you had some questions about James Wierman," he said.

"Yes, just a couple of routine things," I said. "We're trying to determine who was the last person to see him alive yesterday. We thought maybe he had some of the Cabrillo Vo-Tech students helping him. We'd need to talk to them of course."

Malcolm Cross considered my question. "I'm surprised the Coast Guard is involved in this investigation. Isn't it a matter for the San Pedro Police Department?"

"Of course. They're doing the bulk of the investigation, but the Coast Guard does get involved anytime there's a death aboard a merchant ship."

"I understand that, Commander, but I'm surprised that you're personally involved. As a senior Coast Guard officer, you must have more important duties to attend to. It seems to me that this matter could be handled by enlisted personnel, or maybe even an Ensign."

"Well, that's what happens when you don't have somebody screening your calls."

Malcolm Cross drummed his fingers on his desk and hesitated. "I'll check into the Vo-Tech students and have somebody call you with that information."

"Thank you, that would help." I didn't want to press too hard until I could find out more about who Malcolm Cross really was. Still, I had to make this interview believable. "I was curious about why Ms. Stark referred me to you."

Malcolm Cross looked at ease with the question. Probably because he had a good answer.

"It's strictly a matter of liability and deep pockets, Commander. SeaTrans is a major contributor to the Veterans Association. As a matter of fact, we're putting up at least ninety-five percent of the money to renovate the *Balboa Victory*. If a lawsuit were to be filed against the Merchant Marine Veterans Association for the wrongful or negligent death of James Wierman, SeaTrans would surely be named as a party to that suit because the Association doesn't have any money. We're just taking early and substantial action to protect our assets."

"That makes sense."

"The *Balboa Victory* has been a huge liability to us from the very beginning."

"I don't understand."

"Environmentally. The ship is full of asbestos, coated with lead-based paint, and contains a host of other toxic materials banned by the Environmental Protection Agency. That's the primary reason those ships sat in the lay-up fleet for so many years, the cleanup costs exceeded the scrap value."

"Why bother now?"

"The Maritime Administration has to move them because of the environmental hazard they pose to Suisun Bay and Mr. Sheridan has a soft spot in his heart for those old ships. The *Dixie* and the *Balboa* are two of the first ships he operated when he broke into the shipping business years ago. Some guys like to restore old cars or airplanes. Franklin Sheridan likes to restore old ships."

I stood up to signal my satisfaction with his answers. "Thank you for your time, Mr. Cross," I said. "And maybe you could have someone fax the Vo-Tech volunteer hours over to my office."

"I'll do that," he said, shaking my hand. "Good luck with your investigation."

Through the office windows, I had an excellent view of an enormous orange and white petroleum tanker approaching the breakwater entrance. The vessel, full of highly explosive cargo, was being escorted by two Coast Guard Sea Marshal patrol craft with flashing blue lights. We were on the job.

Malcolm Cross looked to see why I was staring. "Quite a view isn't it," he said.

"It certainly is."

"Nothing comes in or out of San Pedro that we can't see from here," Malcolm Cross said. The pugnacious glint in his eye was now tinged with condescending arrogance.

8

Last year before my father died, he told me how proud he was of me for what I'd done with my life. That baffled me because at the time my life was a complete wreck. Elisha had passed away eight months earlier and if that wasn't enough, I was on unpaid leave from the Bureau because my DNA was found inside a dead woman associated with our Boca Raton investigation. I'm still trying to get my head around what my father said, but now I'm starting to understand that he wasn't all that proud of what he'd done with his own life. I once heard him say, "Unfortunately, nothing screws up the system more than an honest politician." Dealing with shifty people like Malcolm Cross everyday must have taken an immense toll on him. When we had that last talk, he looked so wasted and paralyzed with pain. At the time, I thought it was the cancer and medication, but now I believe he was facing the realization that his life had been nothing more than deception and manipulation. He had wealth, power, prestige, and three highly successful sons to carry on the family tradition. Was it worth the price he paid or the regrets he took to the grave?

***

On my way to the Coast Guard base, I found that eastbound traffic on the Vincent Thomas Bridge was backed up and moving at a crawl. When I finally got to the Seaside Avenue exit ramp, I was able to squeeze my car between traffic and the concrete barrier. A truck with a shipping container had taken the 180-degree turn too fast and capsized near the bottom of the ramp. The police officer directing traffic started to reprimand me but when he saw my government license plates he waved me through.

The stack of papers on my desk had grown since last night. Yeoman Jenkins said he'd hold my calls unless it was an emergency and would let me know when it was time to leave for the luncheon. I popped open a Red Bull and attacked the mess on my desk like a man on a mission, destroying so much paper that my shredder motor overheated. About half way through my second trashcan, Yeoman Jenkins knocked on the door and reminded me it was time to leave for the luncheon. After taking a happy pill and using the restroom, I drove back over the Vincent Thomas Bridge to the monthly Harbor Safety Focus Group luncheon that was being held in a side room of the Blue Marlin restaurant on 22nd Street near the marina.

The focus group wasn't my idea. As a matter of fact, nobody with a government job would ever suggest such a ridiculous thing. The focus group was the brainchild of the Pacific Shippers Association, the political entity of the ship owners and operators on the West Coast whose main goal was to keep cargo moving and operating expenses down. By having an open forum on harbor safety, the PSA could get an early indication of prospective harbor security changes and then lobby against things they didn't like while pushing for more favorable treatment. They constantly complained that increased security in California harbors interfered with free trade and made their operations less competitive in the global market.

The Coast Guard's Merchant Vessel Automatic Identification System (MVAIS), more commonly called MAVIS, was the topic at today's luncheon because the system was due to go online within a few months. MAVIS would help the Coast Guard identify and electronically track commercial ships approaching U.S. ports long before they came over the horizon. Members of the focus group complained about the complexity of the system even though similar technology has been used aboard commercial aircraft for years. The Korea Line representative groused that equipment installed aboard his company's ships last year was obsolete due to changes in the system and he would now have to upgrade it at additional expense. A Greek shipowner asked about the possibility of extending the grace period for compliance as well as the procedure to follow if equipment aboard a ship became inoperable at sea between the departure and arrival ports. There were about thirty people at the luncheon and the decorum soon deteriorated into a half dozen or so heated discussions.

Malcolm Cross wasn't at the luncheon, which didn't surprise me because I hadn't seen him at any of the previous events. Still, you would expect someone responsible for public and community relations for a major shipping company to be at a monthly harbor safety luncheon.

The cocktail waitress brought the second round of drinks, and given the noise level in the room, I could see it was going to be a long afternoon at the Blue Marlin. After finishing my crabcake sandwich, I said a few polite goodbyes, slipped out a side door, and returned to the Coast Guard base so I could finish clearing my desk.

By four o'clock the confusion on my desk had been organized into a stack of filing for Yeoman Jenkins to take care of and two pages of prioritized handwritten notes on a yellow legal pad. The first item on my list was the daily ship arrival list. Vessels are required to give at least 72 hours notice before entering San Pedro Harbor so Homeland Security has ample time to assess any threat they may pose. There was only one ship red-flagged for tonight, A Liberian registered freighter coming from Chile with a load of refrigerated fruit. Customs had initiated the red-flag and that usually meant they suspected a discrepancy in the cargo manifests. Sometimes they wanted the Coast Guard to take their boarding team to sea to meet the ship, but a quick phone call to their office indicated they weren't interested and would wait until the ship was securely tied up to the dock. Not that I could blame them. The last time we took one of their boarding teams to sea, eleven out of the twelve Customs officers got seasick. It turns out that green and vomiting Customs officers are not effective Customs officers.

Next week's duty schedule was approved with minor changes, meetings and luncheons entered on my daily planner, and Coast Guard boarding teams were assigned to all tankers and passenger ships due to arrive in the next 72 hours. Yeoman Jenkins grimaced when I showed up with the heap of documents I wanted him to file.

"Brooke Wierman called a couple of times," he said, handing me a stack of pink slips with the phone messages he'd taken. "She also left something on your voice mail."

"Thanks," I said, ducking back into my office. It felt good to be caught up on my paperwork and I was in the mood to go rowing again. The sun didn't set until after seven o'clock this time of year and an afternoon workout would do me good.

Why was Brooke Wierman calling me? I sat at my desk and thumbed through the other messages. Nothing from my boss, Admiral Ballard. That was good. Malcolm Cross hadn't called and none of the other messages were urgent. Maybe I could get away and row after all. But why was Brooke Wierman calling me?

I systematically listened to and then deleted my voice mails until I got to Brooke Wierman's.

She said her father left something in his safety deposit box addressed to the Coast Guard and she didn't know what to do with it. I punched up the phone number she'd left me and she answered on the second ring.

"My mom and I went to the bank to get dad's life insurance policies from the safety deposit box. We found an envelope with some of his other papers and it's addressed to the Coast Guard," Brooke Wierman said. "It wasn't addressed to anyone in particular and we didn't know who to call or where to send it. You left your card last night so I called you."

"What's in the envelope?"

"I don't know," she said. "It's sealed, but it has a note on it that says to make sure the Coast Guard gets it."

"A note?"

"A little yellow sticky note." She paused. "The note says, 'Please forward to the U.S. Coast Guard'."

"What does the envelope say?" I asked, hoping there would be an indication where it should be sent.

"It's just addressed to the U.S. Coast Guard. No name or address, just U.S. Coast Guard." Brooke Wierman sighed into the phone. "What do I do with it?"

A number of thoughts raced through my head but the one that emerged victorious was the idea to pick up the envelope myself and then go rowing as long as I was on that side of town. After finishing my workout, I could stop by the grocery store to do a little shopping and then spend the evening catching up on my laundry.

Brooke Wierman gave me the address, she was still at her mom's house, and I said I'd be there in a half hour. Before leaving the office, I tried calling Malcolm Cross but he wasn't in. I left a message letting him know I still wanted the Cabrillo Vo-Tech volunteer hours. Rachel Terazzo didn't answer her cell phone so I left her a brief message about Brooke Wierman's phone call and the envelope.

The sun greeted me as soon as I stepped outside the back door, its warmth and brightness a pleasant surprise because when I'd returned from lunch the sky was still overcast. The brisk onshore breeze that was whipping the base's American flag was a direct result of the eastern desert heating and drawing the cooler moist air off the ocean. Later, when the sun dropped below the horizon and the desert cooled, the onshore breeze would weaken and die. Then as evening turned to night, the moist sea air trapped over land would drop to its dew point, forming a dense fog that would extend inland for miles.

The *Aegean Centaur,* a fully laden Liberian flagged tanker with a harbor tug made up to her starboard bow, was steaming up the main shipping channel past the Coast Guard base. The Coast Guard's Terminal Island base is strategically located at the east entrance to the one thousand foot wide main shipping channel for Los Angeles and is a collection of World War II era buildings kept current with endless coats of white paint. The extravagant and immaculately kept palm strewn lawns are generally considered a waste of prime harbor real estate worth millions of dollars an acre. The base has its own dock along the main shipping channel that is home to several medium endurance cutters, a buoy tender, and an ice breaker or two when it's too cold to break ice up north. A small vessel facility shoreward of the main dock is home to a number of escort and patrol craft as well as the Coast Guard Sea Marshal Op-Center that's the nucleus of harbor security. Steaming up the channel, the *Aegean Centaur* looked like she had a lot of hard sea miles on her because copious amounts of rust streaked down the sides of her black hull below the deck scuppers. An orange and white forty-foot Coast Guard Sea Marshal patrol boat followed the tanker at a leisurely distance.

***

Brooke Wierman answered the door wearing a white Christian Dior jogging suit that was quite flattering to her figure. The cocktail glass in her right hand looked and smelled like a Manhattan. I noticed that her eyes were a little puffy from crying but her hair and makeup were immaculate and she wore an expensive pearl necklace, a diamond tennis bracelet and several rings, one of which was a pear shaped diamond that had to be over two carats in size.

"Mom's resting right now, but please come in," she said, motioning me inside with her cocktail glass. "Would you like something to drink?"

A Jack and Seven sounded good, but since I was planning to work out, I politely declined. Besides, I was still in uniform and more or less on duty. Not that military men don't occasionally imbibe a little while in uniform or on duty. We retired to the living room where I took a seat on the burgundy leather sofa. Brooke Wierman sat next to me, tucking one leg under her with cat-like grace, her right arm and drink across the back of the sofa as she faced me.

With slightly slurred speech, Brooke Wierman told me all about her day while she sipped her cocktail. She had assumed the responsibility of notifying all the relatives and making the funeral arrangements, and of course, there were so many details to be attended to. I quietly listened as she spent about ten minutes giving me more personal details than I needed to know about her life, marriage, and family. She finally stared at her cocktail glass, somewhat puzzled to find it empty, and then unfolded herself from the sofa. "I'll get that envelope for you."

In a few moments she returned from the kitchen with an eight-by-ten inch manila envelope like the one she had described to me over the phone.

"I should check on Mom," she said, handing me the envelope and a sterling silver letter opener that had an inlaid mother of pearl handle.

After she disappeared down the hall in the direction of the bedrooms, I slit the envelope open and pulled out the four handwritten pages.

July 7, 1995

Coast Guard Officer In Charge,

The purpose of this letter is to set the record straight concerning the sinking of the S.S. SeaTrans Expeditor in the South China Sea on June 12th 1971.

I have said nothing about this incident to anyone, but now, with the death of Captain James Miller, I feel compelled to at least write down the truth.

I joined the SeaTrans Expeditor in San Pedro, California on May 4th, 1971 as Chief Engineer. On May 6th, Captain Miller, the Master of the vessel, and I were summoned to a meeting at the old SeaTrans office on Waterfront Street. This meeting was called by Frank Sheridan, the owner of SeaTrans. We were introduced to Admiral John E. Greenwalt of U.S. Naval Intelligence and then Frank Sheridan left the meeting. Admiral Greenwalt explained to Capt. Miller and myself that the Soviet Navy was tracking our submarines as they operated off the coast of Vietnam. The U.S. Navy had planted devices in the seabed off the coast of Vietnam to interfere with and cover up our submarine's movements but that the Soviets had located and destroyed all of these devices with depth charges. As a result, our submarines were left exposed. He went on to say that the Navy had developed a newer jamming device with greater range and durability. The Navy's plan was to place these devices inside the hulls of derelict ships because the hulls would provide protection from Soviet depth charges and also make the devices harder to locate. They wanted to quietly sink the derelicts in precise locations that would provide a protection grid for our submarine operations. He explained that since the SeaTrans Expeditor was due to be scrapped anyway, the Navy had purchased the ship and was going to install one of the new devices in a cargo hold. Admiral Greenwalt wanted Capt. Miller and myself to scuttle the SeaTrans Expeditor in the South China Sea by pretending we had an engine breakdown and then opening the sea valves that would flood the engineroom and sink the ship. He also stressed to us that this was a Top Secret operation and our confidentiality was vital.

We sailed from San Pedro on May 10th with a load of military cargo, arriving in Pearl Harbor, Hawaii on May 18th. For three days cargo was unloaded and we sailed for Subic Bay, Philippines early May 22nd and arrived on June 2nd.

Admiral Greenwalt came aboard the ship in Subic Bay to give Capt. Miller the location we were to scuttle the ship and our final instructions. He told us how important it was that we not tell anyone of this plan because the Soviets would use any means to prevent success of the operation. He informed us that the Navy would be monitoring our position and would arrange prompt rescue once the ship was scuttled and that under no circumstances were we to broadcast an S.O.S.

or our position. We were not offered nor did we accept any money for what we did. We both felt it was our patriotic duty to serve our country in a time of war.

We sailed from Subic Bay, supposedly bound for Cam Ranh Bay, Vietnam, on the evening of June 10th. After hearing from Captain Miller that we were in the prearranged location, it was on the morning of June 12th that I informed the ship's engineers that there was a leak in the main condenser that was causing both boilers to salt up with seawater. I of course had added seawater to the morning boiler water samples myself. The ship's engineers assisted me as we shut down the turbines and boilers, secured the sea valves, and then pulled the inspection plates off the main condenser that turns the ship's steam back into boiler water. When this was done, I sent everyone on a coffee break before commencing repairs to the main condenser. Once everyone else was clear of the engineroom, I doubled back and opened all the sea valves so the engineroom would flood through the opened condenser. I was sitting in the mess hall with everyone else when the bilge alarm sounded. There was nothing anyone could do to save the ship so Capt. Miller sounded the general alarm and the ship was abandoned in orderly and seamanlike fashion without injury or loss of life. The ship sank in less than thirty minutes. We had done our duty.

After the fact, I had several problems with the incident. First, the Navy did not rescue us. We were left adrift in deteriorating weather conditions in open boats for two days before being rescued by a passing Norwegian freighter. Secondly, no one came to our defense at the Coast Guard inquiry in Honolulu. Captain Miller and I both received six months suspensions on our licenses (with resulting loss of pay since we couldn't work) for gross negligence and only escaped total and permanent revocation of our licenses because several other ships coming out of the layup fleet in Suisun Bay also had a problem with sea valve failure. Finally, upon returning stateside and reporting to SeaTrans, Frank Sheridan fired us both from the company.

Neither Capt. Miller nor I ever said anything to anybody else about this incident. We were questioned by the Federal Bureau of Investigation on numerous occasions and threatened with charges of treason for sabotage of a United States vessel during time of war. We both stuck by the cover story provided to us by Admiral Greenwalt and maintained to the very end that the sinking of the SeaTrans Expeditor was accidental.

Now that Captain James Miller has passed away, I feel the truth should be written down so one day it may come to light.

Respectfully,

James Wierman
Chief Engineer

I placed the letter back in the manila envelope. I was stunned. I hadn't expected something like this. Brooke Wierman was still with her mother so I left the living room and slipped into James Wierman's office. Everything was just the way it was last night. The missing picture frame was more noticeable than ever and I walked over and touched the nail hole again.

"Is everything okay?" Brooke Wierman asked. She poised a fresh cocktail midair with her right hand as she leaned against the doorjamb.

"Fine." It occurred to me that she might wonder what I was doing in her father's office and I briefly considered asking her if she noticed a picture missing from the wall but she spoke first.

"Mother is asleep, are you sure I can't fix you a drink?" she asked.

"I've got to get back to work," I said, feeling a little uneasy. Was she hitting on me or was it my imagination?

"Too bad," she said and then sipped her drink.

I fingered James Wierman's letter.

"Was it anything important?" she asked, using her drink to point at the manila envelope in my hand.

"Not really," I said, tapping the envelope. "Just routine Coast Guard business. But thanks for calling, now we can add this to his permanent record."

9

The Von's supermarket on 25th Street and Western Avenue was chaotic at twenty past five. It was as if everyone in town ran out of food at the same time. The majority of the customers seemed to be working moms with hungry, whiney children fresh from the rigors of daycare. The next largest segment of patrons consisted of retired couples that shuffled along with their shopping carts, blocking the aisles while they discussed and argued the merits of every item before it went into their cart. At the rate they were shopping, they had probably been there for hours and were sure to be obstructing aisles long after I left.

My basket had a nice piece of swordfish with which I intended to make fish tacos. I'd found the white corn tortillas, fresh jalapeno salsa, longhorn cheese, and a six-pack of Coronas, but still needed cilantro, limes, and some Mexican coleslaw if I could find it. As I shopped, the contents of James Wierman's letter kept running through my mind.

The dates on his letter indicated Wierman waited twenty-four years before he wrote it and then it sat in a safety deposit box for more than a decade.   Why hadn't he written and mailed it earlier?   Somewhere along the line he must have figured out that he'd been fucked over. Somebody asked him to keep a secret, and even though they left him to die in an open boat in the South China Sea, he'd kept that secret. If somebody left me in a boat in the middle of the ocean for two days and then fired me after I finally got rescued, I'd be singing like a canary when the FBI questioned me. Why had James Wierman kept the secret for so long?   Was it patriotism or something else? Mrs. Wierman said her husband came home mad as hell a week ago. Wierman helped scuttle the *SeaTrans Expeditor* in 1971 and only recently took a job on the *Balboa Victory* that was being restored with SeaTrans money. Did he finally confront the dying Franklin Sheridan about the sinking of the *SeaTrans Expeditor* after all these years?   What happened after all this time that made him so mad and ultimately got him killed?

A pretty green-eyed redhead in a flowered sundress was in the checkout line ahead of me, unloading her shopping cart as she double-checked to make sure she had everything. Two thick porterhouse steaks hit the conveyor belt, followed by all the fixings and a bottle of Sebastiani's finest Napa Valley Cabernet Sauvignon.   She wasn't wearing a wedding or engagement ring so I jumped to the conclusion that she was trying to get to some man's heart through his stomach.   The last thing she took from her cart was a cherry cheesecake and then she rummaged around in her purse for a checkbook. Some lucky guy was going to have a little more than cherry cheesecake for dessert tonight.

On the way back to my car with the two half-full bags of groceries that cost me a total of $58.52, my cell phone rang. It was Rachel Terazzo.

"You busy?" she asked.

"Not really. Why?"

"We got a tip from the dayshift that some old nautical items have been turning up at Pacific Avenue Pawn and Loan. I thought maybe you wanted to go take a look with me."

"What kind of items?"

"I don't know, but you'd know more about that than I would, you being a sailor and all."

"When?"

"Right now. I'm parked down the block on Pacific Avenue where I can see the front door. I'll wait for you."

"Did you get the message I left you this afternoon?"

"Yeah, what was that all about?"

"It was a letter written by James Wierman before he died."

"What'd it say?"

"You'll have to read it. I'll bring it, give me ten minutes."

"I'll be here."

Last night Lieutenant Richards said the FBI was looking into the death of a security guard on the *Balboa Victory* while it was in the layup fleet in Suisun Bay. He'd also said the fleet layup superintendent suspected someone was looting the ships. Earlier today I'd seen the Cabrillo Vo-Tech students moving metal boxes full of old spare parts. Maybe they'd helped themselves to a few collectibles and then hit the pawnshop to convert their spoils into fun-coupons.

While I drove through traffic, I called the Coast Guard dispatcher on duty and told her I wanted the Sea Marshal harbor patrols to keep a close watch for suspicious activity aboard the *Balboa Victory*. If any looting was going on, we might get lucky.

Rachel was parked a half-block down and across the street from the pawnshop. I drove past her, turned right at the corner, went around the block and then parked several cars behind her on the east side of Pacific Avenue. I pulled the manila envelope from where I'd stashed it over the sun visor, locked my car, worried for a moment if my swordfish would spoil in the trunk, and then walked up the block to her unmarked white Chevrolet Caprice. She jumped when I knocked on the passenger window. The door locks popped open and she motioned me in. The inside of her police car smelled like an old tennis shoe but she had the lingering scent of suntan lotion.

Rachel took the manila envelope from me as I slid into the passenger's seat. She read the letter in silence, stopping several times to go back and look at something on a previous page. When she finished reading it, she slipped it back into the envelope and handed it to me.

"I'd like to get a copy of that for our files," she said.

"Sure. What do you think about the letter?"

"I think there's a helluva lot we don't know."

Rachel watched the front door of the pawnshop without speaking. The pawnshop across the street was near the end of the block, and to the right of it, on the corner, was a longshoreman's bar named the Snatch Block. I'd been there a couple of times. It was a seedy place with liferings, cargo hooks and nets adorning the walls, sawdust on the floor to hide the fact they never swept up. Behind the bar were several dozen framed black and white photographs of picket lines and rioting longshoremen on strike that went hand in hand with the greasy cuisine and buck-and-a-half glasses of draft beer. If you were looking for a cheap place to get drunk and start a fight, the Snatch Block was the place to go.

To the left of the pawnshop was a secondhand clothing store called the Bargain Bin. In front of the Bargain Bin two panhandlers worked the sparse pedestrian traffic on the sidewalk, one of them juggled oranges while the other held out an old cowboy hat to collect tips. Not much of an act at all. They looked like they were in their late twenties or early thirties, a little ragged around the edges, but certainly able-bodied enough to hold down regular jobs if they wanted.

To the left of the Bargain Bin was a small café called Rex's that served killer blueberry pancakes all day and next to it was another clothing store, a little higher end than the Bargain Bin, called

Julie's.   Ned's Drug Emporium occupied the
corner spot at the end of the block.

"What are we doing?" I asked.

"Just watching."

"Watching for what?"

"Just watching."

"Where's you partner today?"

"I don't have a partner."

"You had a partner.   What was his name?
Smith?

"Schmitt. He got another partner." Rachel
continued to stare out her window.   "Nobody
wants to work with me," she said after a moment
of silence.

"Why?"

She turned to face me.   "Usually by the time
guys make detective, they're married."

"So?"

"So, their wives don't want them working with
me."   Behind the frustration in her eyes I could
see she was hurting. "Would your wife want you
working nights with me?" she asked, her voice
dripping with sarcasm.

She probably didn't mean to be cruel, but her
comment cut clean to the bone.   The loss of
Elisha had been devastating to me, and if not for
the bottle of pills I carried in my pocket, I
wouldn't be able to function on a daily basis.

She must have seen it in my eyes.

"Sorry," she said, diverting her attention back
to the front door of the pawnshop.

We sat in the car for several more minutes,
watching the pawnshop, the silence almost
unbearable.

"Maybe you could get a female partner."

"Tried that. Didn't work," she said without looking at me.

I could see the reflection of her face in the side window glass. "Why?"

She snapped her head around and stared straight at me. "What's with all the questions?" Rage welling up behind her brown eyes. "It didn't work, that's all. It just didn't work, it's a long story so let's just drop it."

"Sure."

"Shit," she said, jerking her car door open. "Let's get this over with."

Rachel cut straight across the street, stopping traffic by holding up her hand. Tires squealed. I threw the manila envelope in the seat, locked the car doors, and then ran to keep up.

She charged through the front door of the cluttered pawnshop like a Brahma bull on amphetamines. I'd caught up and was two steps behind her. There was a long glass counter to the left and merchandise was arbitrarily stacked on the floor or hanging from nails in the wall.

Rachel had her weapon drawn in an instant and pointed it at the obese man behind the counter. "Keep your hands where I can see them!"

The man had one hand below the counter but slowly placed both of them on the glass, palms down. Rachel hustled around the counter, keeping her weapon trained on his forehead. She retrieved a magazine he'd hidden.

"Kiddie porn!" she said, slamming the magazine on the counter and holstering her firearm. "You're a sick man, Fat Louie."

"It's not mine," Fat Louie said.

Rachel hit Fat Louie in the head behind his left ear with the heel of her right hand. "Don't give me your bullshit, Louie, you're on parole. They'll lock you up and throw away the key."

"You're violating my rights, this is an illegal search!"

Rachel smacked Fat Louie again. "I don't need a search warrant, this was in plain sight you asshole."

"Quit hitting me," whined Fat Louie. He looked at me, his jowls quivered, sweat glistened on his brow. "Make her quit hitting me."

Fat Louie was a pitiful piece of work.

Rachel began searching behind the counter.

"You can't do that," Fat Louie said. "You don't have a search warrant."

Rachel pulled a cardboard box full of magazines from under the counter and threw it on the floor.

"You're going away for a long, long time, Louie," she said. "You know what they do to guys like you in the big house?"

"Those aren't mine, I swear!" Fat Louie was really sweating now. "Some guy brought those in, they're not mine."

"Yeah, well they're in your possession and you're already on parole, not to mention you're a registered sex offender. You're going to jail."

"You can't do this."

Rachel shoved Fat Louie. "Move your ass."

When Fat Louie came from behind the counter I could see he stood about five-ten and went a good 400 pounds. He wore huge khaki pants, white canvas boating shoes, and a baggy Hawaiian shirt with sweat rings in the armpits.

"We can work this out, give me a break, some guy left those here, I told him to come and get them, I'd get in trouble," blubbered Fat Louie. "They're not mine, I swear!"

"Shut up, scumbag." Rachel hit Fat Louie in the back of the head with the palm of her hand one more time.

Fat Louie whimpered.

"You took in some nautical memorabilia in the last couple of days," Rachel said. "This guy is from the Coast Guard and he wants to see it."

"The only stuff I have is what you see here," Fat Louie said.

There were some glass fishing floats on the wall, a few international-orange liferings with ship names stenciled on them, some old wooden cheek blocks used for cargo gear, and a couple of wooden ships wheels that were mixed in with the usual pawnshop guitars, amplifiers, stereos, speakers, shop tools, small appliances, and portable air conditioners.

"Don't fuck with me with me, Louie," Rachel said raising a hand. "I know it's here!"

Fat Louie cowered. "All right, all right. I've got some stuff in the back, I was going to call you guys."

"I'll bet," Rachel said.

Fat Louie barely fit through the door to the cramped back room. A light bulb hung over a metal desk littered with paper, several open bags of potato chips, and wadded up Twinkie wrappers. Shelves lined the walls, floor to ceiling, and were crammed with cardboard boxes of varying sizes. A grimy toilet sat in one corner, a filthy sink next to it. The place smelled like stale sweat odor and rancid urine. Fat Louie shuffled over and pulled two large boxes from a shelf, letting them hit the floor with a thud. Rachel motioned for him to step away and I went over to see what was in the boxes.

The first box had three marine sextants in their original wooden cases, six Hamilton wind-up chronometers, and an assortment of brass dividers used for navigation. The second box contained about a dozen brass ship's clocks.

Rachel walked over. "What do you think?"

"This stuff came off ships all right. We'll have to get the serial numbers and then see if the Maritime Administration still has a record of what they put on each ship." I paused and looked through the boxes again. "We might get lucky and be able to track it back to a specific ship. But then again, all this stuff is pretty old, so..."

"Where'd you get it, Louie, and don't make me smack you again," Rachel said. She stood squarely in front of Fat Louie with her hands on her hips and her feet spread shoulder width.

Fat Louie looked nervous.

Rachel raised her hand to hit him.

"Okay, okay. It was that retarded kid. I buy stuff from him all the time."

"What retarded kid?" Rachel asked.

"He works down on the fishing boats, rides that bicycle with the trailer behind it." Fat Louie was sweating buckets, stinking up the back room.

"Eddie Canetti?" asked Rachel.

"Yeah, Eddie," Fat Louie said. "He comes in here all time with stuff."

Everybody in San Pedro knew Eddie Canetti. He was more than a kid, probably in his mid-twenties, pleasant, and rode his bike around town collecting cans and bottles for the recycling center. His uncle owned a fishing boat and Eddie would hang around the fish pier doing odd jobs on fishing boats for money. He was definitely a little slow on the uptake, but everybody liked him and sometimes gave him things they were going to throw out anyway. However, what Fat Louie had in the boxes wasn't junk.

"Where does he get it?"

"I don't know. He rides his bike around and goes through the trash, or finds stuff that washes up on the beach." Fat Louie's eyes darted around the room; sweat ran down his jowls. "I don't know."

"You're trying to tell me that Eddie found a bunch of brass clocks washed up on the beach?" Rachel said.

"I don't know where he got them," Fat Louie stuttered. "But he never brings me nothing that's stolen."

Rachel looked at the contents of the boxes again. "How much did you give him for this stuff?" she asked.

"I don't remember."

Rachel thumped Fat Louie again. This time with her left hand. He tried to raise his arms to block the blow but she was too quick.

"How much, Louie?"

"Two hundred."

Rachel looked at me. "What's it worth?"

The sextants were in good shape and very collectable. The chronometers and clocks were antique and pristine. "I don't know, depends on where you sell them," I said, doing the math in my head. "In the right market, all of it would be worth about ten or twelve thousand dollars. Maybe more."

"You gave him two hundred bucks?" Rachel feigned a backhand and Fat Louie covered up. "Well, you're out two hundred bucks, shitbird. We're taking this as evidence."

"What do you mean evidence?" Fat Louie protested.

"Stolen merchandise."

"It's not stolen!"

"Prove it."

"You gotta give me a receipt."

"No problem." Rachel said.

We took the boxes out of the backroom and Rachel gave Fat Louie a handwritten receipt on a piece of scratch paper she got from the counter. "Get rid of the kiddie porn, Louie. When I come back, I'm coming back looking, and if I find any kiddie porn, I'll burn this fucking shithole to ground with you in it."

Fat Louie's face was red and sweat ran down the back of his neck behind his ears, but he didn't speak. He could only force several quick nods of his head.

Rachel carried one box across the street and I carried the other. We slid them into the back seat of her car.

"I'm surprised you didn't arrest him."

"Arrest Fat Louie?" she said. "Every two-bit crook in town fences through Fat Louie and then they head next door to the bar to have a few drinks and brag about how smart they are. We give the bartenders ten bucks for every tip that's good. They have big ears and probably get more money from us than they do tending bar. If we locked Fat Louie up, the department wouldn't solve a tenth of the burglaries in this town. Fat Louie is a disgusting piece of dog shit, but at least we know what we're dealing with and how to make him talk."

"Do you need any more help?"

"No. I'll run the serial numbers and check with the Maritime Administration, " Rachel said. "And maybe the Veteran's Association here in town or the superintendent up in Suisun Bay might know if something's missing."

"Sounds good."

Rachel paused, looking me in the eye. She had something else to say but was having trouble finding words.

"Well, I'm off to protect and serve," she said, finally. "That's our motto. Protect and serve."

"Good luck with that," I said, turning to walk to my car.

"Jared."

I looked over my shoulder. She had the manila envelope containing James Wierman's letter.

"Don't forget this," she said.

"Thanks."

"Jared, I'm really sorry about what I said. I didn't mean anything by it, it just came out wrong."

There was really nothing to say. I shrugged it off and went to my car. By the time I'd unlocked the door and climbed behind the wheel, Rachel Terazzo was gone.

10

A relaxing evening spent rowing my scull around the harbor was out of the question now. Rachel's comment about my wife and then the encounter with Fat Louie at the pawnshop put me in a foul mood. My guts were in turmoil and I had feelings that needed repressing. Fortunately, I knew just how to do it.

Both the restaurant and the bar at the Harbor Light were packed. My usual corner seat was taken, which seemed particularly irritating to me this evening for some reason, so I grabbed an open barstool at the far end of the lounge near the kitchen door.

Stan was swamped with drink orders from the restaurant but managed to bring me my usual, scurrying away to attend to someone else further down the bar without speaking or taking my money.

Little white pills and Tennessee sour-mash whiskey. A sure cure for whatever ails you. Rachel's comment had unleashed a whole pack of mongrel dogs that were eating m guts from the inside out and I was going to have a hell of a time getting them quieted down again.

She had apologized and I'm sure she didn't make the comment to be cruel. How was she supposed to know? She knew Elisha died, I'd told her that much, but I hadn't told her about my affair with Monique Latrelle.

The first drink was already half gone, scarcely dulling the memories of the affair that was as fresh as if it had happened just this afternoon, so I waved Stan down to order a backup.

"Bad day, Commander?" Stan quipped.

"You have no idea." The noise in the Harbor Light was annoying me. Plates and silverware banging, people laughing, talking way too loud. Can't a guy just get shitfaced in peace?

At first, the undercover assignment in Boca Raton seemed like a dream come true. All I had to do was hobnob with the rich and famous while doing a little surveillance work. Homeland Security was tracking financial transactions for some of the more prominent movers and shakers in southern Florida, the nouveaux riche in particular, trying to detect any irregularities that might indicate they were funding terrorist organizations or laundering drug money. The Bureau developed a cover for me as a trust fund baby that had inherited over 300 million from the sale of my family's real estate holdings and Pittsburgh steel mill. I was set up in a sprawling mansion on a Boca canal with an 86-foot Burger motor yacht parked at the dock out back to complete of the illusion. On the surface, it appeared that I spent my time managing trust fund investments, but in fact, I was just shuffling the same money from account to account. My assignments took from me Florida to offshore banks in the Caribbean as well as some of the prominent cities in Europe. It was all show, just moving the same money from place to place so I could develop banking contacts and let the other wealthy investors see my face in their environment.

It takes more than money to infiltrate the sphere of wealth because in reality it's a small world where the players make it their business to know one another. The nouveaux riche are especially suspect and held in low regard by the old-money people. However, be it old money or new money, the wealthy have two traits that are common to them, and if manipulated, can become weaknesses. Greed and paranoia. Since they never have enough money, they plot to capture yours while worrying about how you're going to get your hands on theirs.

After I'd been in Boca Raton for a few months and my presence pretty well established, Homeland Security developed a primary interest in Andre Latrelle. He couldn't be classified as either old or new money, his grandfather had started an import and export business in Marseilles after World War Two. In the spring of 2004, Andre took over the reigns of Chevoix Internationale, the family business that was well-founded in the Mediterranean area, and once in charge, he quickly expanded to the Caribbean and southern Florida areas. Andre Latrelle's dealings in both Tunisia and Algeria, probably initially developed by his grandfather, were of particular interest to Homeland Security.

Unlike movie stars that vacation in areas where they are most likely to be seen and are sure to be photographed, the wealthy and powerful like their privacy. You won't find them taking a leisurely stroll along a beach in Cancun and when you see them, you can't just walk up and introduce yourself, asking them for an autograph or inquire about their astrological sign. According to intelligence reports, Andre Latrelle frequented a secluded private resort in the San Blas Islands off Panama. Properly timed, I cruised the 86-foot Burger motor yacht by the resort while he was there, anchored for lunch, and then spent an hour or so snorkeling. Three weeks later, we passed as I was leaving a private bank in Geneva and he was coming in. The next month, I made an appearance at the elite and extremely private Lac Lapeyrere north of Marseille where he was dining with his daughter, Monique. Our chance encounters were enough to make him curious, but not enough to make him paranoid. Intelligence confirmed he checked my background.

Monique was a wild child, twenty-four, ten years younger than I was at the time, and liked to spend her evenings in the haut-monde clubs in New York and Miami, partying with the celebrity crowd. Since her father kept her as close to him as was humanly possible for a father to do with a tempestuous twenty-four year old daughter, it was decided she was my best avenue to access him. The initial introduction in New York was arranged by the Bureau through a friend of a friend of hers, a model named Georgette Reece that was trying to clear herself of some inconvenient cocaine charges. Georgette walked into the club on my arm, we danced, and then she introduced me. Monique and I talked briefly that first night, but nine days later in Monaco, I was invited to her dinner table for a drink and afterward we played roulette, losing quite badly and laughing about it. I was rich, good-looking, and funny, with an air of maturity. I was the perfect boyfriend. Or so it seemed.

Needless to say, Elisha was not pleased that I was spending so much time away from her. The sole purpose of me leaving the Coast Guard in the first place was so we would have more quality time together. The Bureau was good about giving me days off, but I had no regular schedule and we could never plan anything beforehand. I would show up at odd hours, any day of the week, and then would be called away on short notice. I was preoccupied, I told her, because of the stress, and yes, I said, I'd requested a transfer, although I hadn't. Towards the end, I sometimes passed up the chance to go home and often avoided calling her in order to dodge the arguments that were becoming more heated, a loud and clear signal that our relationship was in trouble.

Although I loved Elisha dearly, I thoroughly enjoyed the pampered and privileged life that was my undercover assignment. On one occasion, Monique slipped away from her father and met me in Tortola, British Virgin Islands, and we spent several days on the yacht. I was supposed to be checking out a condominium investment there, as part of my cover story of course, but we spent ample time together. She was a tigress in bed, uninhibited, and showed me a few things I'd never seen. On top of all that, she was forbidden fruit, and that made the affair particularly exhilarating.

It was all part of the job. At least that's what I rationalized to myself. Besides, there were eight other people present at the meeting when the Bureau decided I should make contact with Andre Latrelle through his daughter. I was following orders. I managed to keep the two worlds, my marriage to Elisha and the affair with Monique, separate until the end.

As Andre Latrelle's business expanded in southern Florida, he stepped on toes. Very vengeful toes. As a sign for Latrelle to back off, something was taken from him, something he loved dearly. His daughter. She'd spent the night with me in Boca Raton, and ten minutes after I dropped her off so I could fly home to spend some time with Elisha, she was ritualistically murdered inside her father's house. The investigation by the Coral Gables Police Department showed that I was the last known person to see her alive, and of course, my DNA was everywhere- under her fingernails, in her hair, inside her. My two worlds collided with a horrific explosion that left me to face Elisha with the truth and a suspension from the Bureau pending a complete investigation. The integrity of the undercover operation had been compromised and irreparable harm done. I'm not sure how many phone calls my father made to bail me out of that jam, but eventually I was allowed to leave the Bureau and return to a new job with the Coast Guard.

Now I was just like everyone else in the world. I was busting my hump at a pain-in-the-ass job that barely paid enough money to cover the bills I'd never get out from under while trying to live down my past and recover from the stupid mistakes I'd made.

My glass was empty and Stan was at the other end of the bar when I felt a hand on the inside of my left thigh.

"I've got something you might be interested in," somebody cooed into my left ear.

Beverley Christy, the manager of the Harbor Light, had taken the stool next to me and I was so busy feeling sorry for myself that I hadn't noticed her arrival.

"What's that?" I asked, jiggling the ice in my glass, then sucking up the negligible amount of whiskey flavored water left behind.

Beverly rubbed my thigh and smiled. She wore an expensive white silk blouse, a dark blue two-pocket skirt, and enough perfume to make my eyes burn.

Stan had apparently seen her walk in because he had her drink on the bar, a gin and tonic with a cherry instead of a slice of lime. I nodded and Stan hit me again, my third drink.

"Are you interested?" she asked, sipping her drink, smiling with her eyes.

"Depends on what you're talking about."

"What do you think I'm talking about?"

Beverly was quite a bit older than my thirty-eight years. I wasn't sure exactly how old she was, plastic surgery and sufficient makeup did wonders, and she appeared to take care of herself. But her reputation had preceded her so there were plenty of places I wasn't about to go with her.

"Well?" she asked, her hand inching up my thigh.

I stabbed at the ice cubes in my glass with the plastic straw. "Let's hear it."

She leaned closer and whispered in my ear, "I think I found you a house."

"What?"

She took her hand off my thigh and slapped me playfully on the shoulder. "A house, silly. What did you think I was talking about?" She sipped her drink and laughed.

Beverly proceeded to tell me about the 92-year old woman in Redondo Beach that was being admitted to a nursing home. The woman had a four-bedroom, two-bath house in a nice 1960's era neighborhood and had outlived her husband and children. A niece living in New Jersey, the daughter of the woman's youngest sister, had been given power of attorney. The niece didn't have time, nor was she willing, to come to California to sort out the details. Beverly had received the phone call and the niece wanted the house sold as soon as possible to cover the nursing home expenses.

"I shot her a lowball figure of what the house was worth and she was happy with it," Beverly said. "It's at least two hundred thousand below market value."

About six months earlier I had the bright idea to buy a house instead of wasting my money on rent. Since Beverly was in the real estate business, one night in the bar, after we'd had a few drinks of course, I mentioned to her that I was in the market and asked her to keep an eye out for something economical. But it didn't take me long to figure out that Southern California homes were out of my price range, especially on Coast Guard pay. Local real estate was a game you had to get into years ago, when the price of admission was more reasonable. If you weren't in the game now and didn't have at least two incomes and a substantial down payment, you were on the outside without a chance of getting in.

"You'll need to move fast," Beverly said. "It won't be on the market long."

Stan was mixing a drink, looking over his shoulder at me with a horrified look on his face. He saw me glance his way and he shook his head ever so slightly, quickly checking to make sure Beverly hadn't seen him give his opinion.

"I don't know," I said. "Somehow it just doesn't seem right to cheat a little old lady out of two hundred thousand dollars."

"Don't be so self-righteous," Beverly said, eating her cherry. "If you don't take it, somebody else will. I'd do it myself, but I have too many deals in the pipeline right now. I thought maybe I'd throw this one to a friend." Beverly put her hand back on my thigh and smiled. "We could work something out."

That's about the time Reverend Johnny walked into the bar. He was wearing his fatigues and fingerless gloves, carrying his coffee can full of money.

Beverly came off her barstool like a Tasmanian Devil-dog.

"Get out of here," she screamed.

Reverend Johnny protested, showing her his money.

"I don't care!" Beverly wailed and shoved Johnny. "You're stinking up the place."

The other patrons in the bar were slack-jawed and Stan came from behind the bar to help Beverly. The wide-eyed blonde hostess from the restaurant came into the bar to see what was going on.

"Call the police," Beverly screamed to the hostess.

Reverend Johnny wasn't leaving. "God sets the lowly on high, and those who mourn are lifted to safety. He thwarts the plans of the crafty so their hands achieve no success."

"Shut up and get out," Beverly screamed.

Stan had Reverend Johnny by the arm and was trying to wrestle him toward the door.

"He catches the wise in their craftiness and the schemes of the wily are swept away," Reverend Johnny said. "Darkness comes upon them in the daytime and at noon they grope as in the night. So the poor have hope and injustice shuts its mouth."

"Get him out of here," Beverly said to Stan.

Stan kept shoving Reverend Johnny towards the door but Johnny was resisting.

"The light shines in the darkness, but the darkness has not understood it," Reverend Johnny said as Stan finally forced him out the front door and onto the sidewalk.

"Shit." Beverly climbed back on her barstool and drained her drink. "Shit."

Stan came back and assumed his position behind the bar. "I got rid of him."

"Good. Make sure he stays out. "Beverly displayed her empty glass to Stan. "I don't want to see that asshole in this place again!"

Stan asked me if I wanted another drink but I waved him off. I'd had enough excitement for the day.

"You know what pisses me off?" Beverly said, turning to me as I finished off my drink.

"What's that?"

"That guy's a fake," she said. "I saw him last year at a restaurant on Santa Monica pier and he was all dressed up. He's too lazy to work so he hangs around here looking for handouts, wearing that phony Army get-up of his." She stirred her new drink with the cherry. "He's a fake."

***

The wrought iron security gate to the parking lot of the Bonita Apartments rolled open and let me drive in. Both of my parking spaces were empty so I knew the Reynoza brothers probably didn't have much of a party going on yet. My groceries were in the trunk and had tipped over during the drive so I had to re-bag them. I smelled my piece of swordfish to make sure it hadn't gone bad, and then with one bag in each arm, I locked my car and walked to the elevator. I'd pressed the button and was waiting for the elevator to arrive when I saw motion from the shadows to my left. Just as my eyes scanned in that direction, the first blow hit me in the back of the head, a thud like a sledgehammer hitting an anvil and then the world went white. My knees had buckled and I was on my way to the concrete when the second blow turned out the lights and sent me within spitting distance of the Promised Land.

11

Julio Reynoza was in my face speaking gibberish. The light was blindingly bright, Julio kept talking, and I suddenly became aware that I was on my back. Panic swept over me and I tried to hit Julio but my right arm wasn't responding.

"Take it easy, man, it's me," Julio said. "I called the cops and they'll be here any minute."

It felt like an axe had been buried in the back of my skull and when I touched it, it was warm and sticky. Julio helped me sit up. I vomited. The blonde girl screamed. My stomach was trying to turn itself inside out and my head swooned, there was no sensation of which way was up, so I dropped back to the concrete, resting in the vomit and blood.

Bad things happen when the brain is slammed against the inside of a person's skull. I'd been there before. The first time was when I was on the Coast Guard rowing team. We were skylarking in the boathouse after a race when I ran into a low wooden beam, peeling my scalp back and knocking myself to my knees. Scalp wounds bleed a lot. I got twelve stitches and a concussion that kept me off the rowing team for two weeks. The second time I split my head open was on a Coast Guard seizure of a Cuban fishing vessel off the coast of Florida. I rushed from the brilliant daylight into the pitch-black fish hold, expecting to find drugs, illegal aliens, or illicit arms, but instead found a steel hatch-coaming with my forehead.

In the movies when someone gets knocked out, they stand up, shake their head a few times, and then resume whatever they were doing. In real life, once the brain has shut down because of trauma, it can take from minutes to several days for the brain to reestablish neuro-pathways that have been interrupted, and sometimes it's weeks, months or even years before everything returns to normal. If it ever does.

I vomited again. My sense of smell came back online and I tried to move away from the stench but could only muster a spasmodic roll.

"Take it easy, man," Julio said.

The blonde girl was screaming and the pain from her screams was as bad as the axe in my head.

"Shut her up," I said, my tongue slow and thick.

"Go get some towels," he told her. "And call the cops again."

I tried sit up again. "Is that my blood?"

"You're going to be all right," Julio said, his eyes wide, near panic.

"I need to lay down," I said. The world was spinning like a merry-go-round but the concrete was cool and felt good. Julio put something under my head and I closed my eyes.

Someone was touching my face, shining a flashlight in my eyes so I lashed out, my arms working better, but there was still no sting to my punches, and then my arms and shoulders were pinned to the ground.

"Sir, can you hear me? Sir?"

"Of course I can hear you, I'm not deaf. Leave me alone."

"We're going to take you to the hospital."

"I'm fine. Leave me alone." I just wanted to sleep.

"Sir, look at me. Can you tell me your name?"

When I opened my eyes the light was unbearable so I closed them again.

"Sir, can you tell me your name?"

"His name is Jared Stanton."

"I know who he is, I want to know if he knows who he is."

"Leave me alone!"

I woke up a couple of times on the ambulance ride and then people were shining light in my eyes again and asking me questions that made absolutely no sense.

It was quiet and the bed was comfortable. Someone touched my shoulder and whispered, "Can you hear me?"

The smell of coconut oil made me open my eyes. It was Rachel Terazzo. "Can you turn some of those lights out?" I said to her.

She left, there was a click and I was able to see.

"The doctor's going to have to turn the lights on when he stitches you up."

"No stitches."

"You need stitches."

"No stitches."

"Argue with the doctor," she said. "Do you know what happened?"

"I'm thirsty."

A plastic cup was being placed to my lips and I slurped, the moisture quenching the arid interior of my mouth.

"More?" she asked.

I took more and my tongue felt better.

"What happened?" she asked.

"I don't know."

The lights came on and a nurse came in. "I need to shave your wound," she announced.

"No."

"I need to shave you so the doctor can put the stitches in."

"No stitches."

"You need stitches."

Like a wounded animal, I snarled and lashed out when she came near me.

"I'll tell the doctor," said the nurse when she decided I wasn't going to let her shave any part of my head.

"You need stitches," Rachel said in a soothing voice.

"I want to go home."

"They want to keep you overnight. You've got a severe concussion."

"I'm going home," I tried to get out of bed only to discover I was wearing a hospital gown that was wide-open in the back, leaving my butt to hang out in the breeze.

Rachel put her hand on my shoulder and said in a low voice, "Let me talk to them."

Rachel spoke to the doctor in the hallway outside my room, I could hear them murmuring, and then he examined me again. I closed my eyes against the light.

Rachel touched my shoulder again and whispered in my ear. "I got you some clothes, you need to get dressed, I'll take you home."

Rachel and the nurse dressed me in sweat pants and a zip-up sweatshirt, slid my leather uniform shoes on my feet without socks, and got me into a wheelchair. My eyes were shut tight against the intense light in the hallway and it wasn't until we were in the parking lot where it was dark that I could open my eyes. With Rachel's help, I struggled out of the wheelchair and slipped into the front seat of her car.

"You're a lousy patient," she said as she started the car. "The only reason they let you come with me was they didn't want to put up with your bullshit."

My eyes were closed during the entire trip; the headlights from the oncoming cars were unbearable. Rachel tried to talk to me while she drove. Sometimes I had answers, sometimes I didn't.

"Here we are," she said. The car came to a halt and the engine shut off.

We were in an alley behind a white stucco apartment building, parked amongst a long row of cars sitting parallel to the building under a matching canopy that gave minimal protection from the sun and rain.

"This isn't where I live," I said.

"Whoever did this to you took your keys, we can't get into your apartment," she said. "This is my place."

"I want to go home."

"You're locked out. It's my place or the hospital."

Rachel had never showed me where she lived so I was going to have to take her word for it. My head hurt too much for me to argue with her, and since she'd gone to the trouble to spring me from the hospital, I decided to go with the flow. When she helped me from the car, I was wobbly and weak.

She led me through a locked gate into the generous pool area that formed the center of the apartment complex. The pool compound was landscaped with lush palm trees and flowers, umbrella tables and barbeque grills were scattered in the corners, reclining pool chairs were everywhere. People were splashing in the blue water of the lighted swimming pool, laughing and talking, but I didn't venture more than a glance, Rachel had me by the arm and I was walking like a drunk.

Fortunately, we only had to climb one flight of stairs and then Rachel was fumbling for her keys, cursing under her breath. She unlocked the door, reached in for the light switch and said, "Come on in."

There was a lamp on in her living room but she left her bedroom dark. I crawled onto her bed and assumed a fetal position on my right side, but that put weight on my scalp wound so I rolled over onto my left side and curled my knees to my chest. Her scent was on the bed and the fragrance transported me, lightly, like a butterfly on the breeze, through the recesses of my mind to nowhere in particular, leaving me with a vague sense of Déjà vu. I could hear her moving around the apartment and it made me feel comfortable and safe, like a small child in bed listening to his parents talk softly in the next room late at night.

"Close your eyes," Rachel said. "I'm turning a light on."

She opened a window and I could hear the surf, a cool breeze tickled me and I hadn't realized until then how stuffy the room was.

"I need to clean up that cut," she announced. "They didn't get to it at the hospital because you threw a fit. This might hurt."

Rachel washed the blood away with warm water and a cloth. "It doesn't look too bad," she said after a minute or so. "How do you feel?"

"Like I'm drunk and hung over all at the same time."

"This is going to sting a little."

It stung a lot.

"It's like a combination of my worst tequila and worst gin hangover combined all into one."

"You'll live," she said. "You need to keep pressure on this if you can." Rachel gently took my hand and held it on the bandage she'd placed over my cut.

The bedroom light went out and then I could hear her talking on the phone. A little while later I could hear a knock on the front door.

"How is he?"

The voice belonged to Lieutenant Richards.

"Not bad right now, if he doesn't get worse in the next twelve hours he'll probably be okay."

It felt like I was floating, the pain grew farther away, the sound of the surf and the cool breeze drifted through the open window, Rachel and Lieutenant Richards murmured in the next room. I tried to focus on what they were saying but kept drifting off. I heard them mention James Wierman and Fat Louie.

"How're you feeling, Commander?" asked Lieutenant Richards.

I hadn't heard him come into the room and his voice startled me.

"Not bad," I said.

"That's good," he said. "You're lucky."

"Yeah, I feel lucky." I had my back to him and was still in a fetal position with my right hand holding the bandage to my head.

"Rachel told me about James Wierman's letter," he said.

The synapses in my brain fired, randomly, searching for what he was talking about. Finally I found it. "Yeah, what about it?"

"Do you remember what you did with it?"

More synapses firing, looking hither and yon in my brain for the memory. This one was taking longer.

"Commander Stanton?"

"I left it in my car over the sun visor."

"We looked in his car," Rachel said. "It wasn't there. The witness said he saw somebody in the car when he and his girlfriend pulled into the garage."

"Okay, Commander," said Lieutenant Richards. "Get some rest, you'll be safer here if you don't mind staying until you're back on your feet."

I wasn't sure what he meant about being safer, but I was comfortable right now as sure as hell and wasn't about to go anywhere.

They left the room and Lieutenant Richards said something else about Fat Louie before I heard the front door close. Rachel talked on the phone for a few minutes and then came into the room to check on me.

"Keep pressure on this," she said, gently pressing on my hand with her fingers.

The sound of the surf was a lullaby that whisked me to a white sand beach. Azure water tickled the alabaster strand that stretched from horizon to horizon, palm trees swaying in the breeze behind me. Penguins frolicked in foamy waves that raced up the beach to kiss sand castles.

Rachel Terazzo left her apartment without me hearing her go.

12

Penguins and palm trees?

My tongue was as thick as a bratwurst and my mouth dry as sawdust. Lying on my left side, arms crossed against my chest with knees drawn up to my chin, I shivered against the cold. When I couldn't stand it any longer, I stumbled from the bed and closed the window, shutting the sound of the surf out of the room, then crumpled back to bed and pulled the covers over me.

Going back to sleep would have been nice but my throat was parched and the throbbing in my head was unmerciful. Sharp stabbing pains between my shoulder blades and a stiff neck invaded my consciousness, finally convincing me I wasn't going back to sleep. I rolled out of bed and headed for the light of the living room but stubbed my toe and stumbled over something. Fortunately, I was able to catch myself with a hand against the wall before I hit the floor.

The inside of Rachel's refrigerator looked a lot like mine, except she had a case of bottled water on the bottom shelf of hers. I took one of the plastic bottles, struggled with the cap, and then drank deeply, the icy wetness stinging and lubricating my throat on the way down. For some reason there was a bitter metallic aftertaste in my mouth. I made a sour face, grabbed a blue plastic pitcher full of orange juice from the top shelf, and then kicked the refrigerator door closed with my foot.

Looking for something to pour the orange juice in, I discovered there wasn't much in the kitchen cabinets. The one next to the stove contained a minimal amount of food; there were some cheap boxes of macaroni and cheese, a couple of cans of tuna fish in spring water, an open box of saltine crackers, a small jar of sweet pickles, an open bag of barbeque potato chips, a variety of instant noodles in styrofoam cups, a can of Spam, and an unopened package of Oreo cookies.

I found the dishes in a cabinet next to the sink, and again, there was a minimal assortment of odds and ends for glasses, cups, and plates. I picked out a coffee cup that said, 'LIFE'S A BITCH AND THEN YOU DIE' because at the moment it seemed appropriate. I filled the cup with orange juice, left the pitcher on the counter, and went back to the living room to sit on the couch. The couch was a tattered plaid piece with turned up cushions, the kind of thing you might find at a second hand furniture store for about fifty bucks. Rachel had a small television set with rabbit ears in the corner on a table and across from the couch, along the far wall, was an open roll top desk with stacks of mail accumulating on it. The only other semi-living thing in the room was a three-foot tall Ficus tree in a five-gallon bucket. It looked about as dead as I felt.

I swigged the orange juice. It tasted like hazardous waste and when I smelled it, there was an overpowering aroma of fermentation so I ended up pouring it down the kitchen sink.

Looking for the bathroom, I discovered that Rachel had a two-bedroom apartment. The door to the other bedroom was open and it had a stationary bike, two large rubber balls, a weight bench, an assortment of dumbbells, and two exercise mats. A single poster of a posing male body builder in all his steroid enhanced glory, flexing his biceps, abdominals, and quadriceps, was taped to the wall in front of the stationary bike.

The bathroom was clean, like the rest of the apartment, but had cosmetics strewn around the sink. A blow-dryer hung on a hook next to the light switch. I ran the water in the sink until it was cold, scooped some into my hand and tried it. It, too, had a metallic taste. Must be me. I rinsed my face with cold water and then paused to consider the blurry image of myself in the mirror. There was a dull cast to my eyes, probably not helped by the gray bags under them, and there was a three inch square piece of folded-up gauze stuck in my hair on the back of my head. I probed the gauze with my fingers, dried blood was holding it in place, and then scrutinized the red smudges on my fingertips from the still seeping wound. It was tempting to look through the medicine cabinet, but respect for Rachel's privacy won out over curiosity.

When I flipped on the bedroom light to find out what I'd tripped over earlier, I discovered two large soft-sided suitcases on the floor. They were both unzipped so I lifted one open with my foot and found it full of neatly folded clothes. The louvered accordion closet doors were open and other than two military dress uniforms, three LAPD uniforms in dry cleaner plastic bags, a red dress, a black cocktail dress, and a long blue sequined gown, the closet was empty. Shoes formed a neat pile next to the suitcases.

I switched off the bedroom light out, assumed the fetal position on the bed again, and pressed the bloody gauze to my scalp.

The next time I woke up and walked into the living room, Rachel was reclining on the couch. She must have been awake because as soon as I came into the room she looked up at me.

"You're alive," she said. "How do you feel?"

"Like shit."

"Good. That means you're getting better."

"Great."

"Are you hungry?"

"Not really."

"Good," she said, swinging her legs to the floor and standing up. "I picked up a few things on the way home. You eat bacon and eggs don't you?"

"I'm not really hungry."

"But you're not sick to your stomach," she said, walking over to look at my eyes and inspect the gauze stuck in my hair. "You need to eat. Coffee?"

"Sure."

There was a small oval faux-wood table shoved against the wall in the kitchen area. Three cheap black plastic and chrome metal swivel chairs were pushed flush with the table. I pulled one out and sat down. It was even more uncomfortable than it looked.

Rachel brought me coffee in a cup that had a picture of two kittens on it and then she opened the vertical blinds covering a sliding glass door. Outside the door was a small patio that overlooked the beach across the street.

"It's probably too cold to eat out there," she said.

There was green outdoor carpet on the patio deck and a small white plastic table with two matching plastic chairs. From the kitchen table, I could see that a misty gray dawn was breaking and that the even grayer ocean was throwing white spray skyward when the surf broke onto the beach.

"Nice view," I said, sipping my coffee that also had a faint metallic taste. I noticed a band-aid on the inside of my right forearm and pulled it off, revealing a purple and red bruise the size of a quarter. Putting two and two together, I figured that the metallic taste in my mouth was from something they'd given me intravenously at the hospital last night.

Rachel took the band-aid from me. "Why live in Southern California if you can't live at the beach?"

After throwing the band-aid in the trash under the sink and washing her hands, Rachel began dropping strips of bacon into a large black cast iron skillet.

"How do you like your eggs?"

"However you're having yours."

"I don't eat eggs," she said.

"Then do whatever's easiest."

Birds were working the edge of the surf across the street, trying to make a living from whatever washed in with the waves. Rachel made fresh orange juice in the blue plastic pitcher and then broke eggs into a skillet sizzling with butter. The toaster popped and she put two more pieces of bread into it. The smell of bacon frying sparked my appetite and then I was suddenly overcome with grief at the loss of Elisha.

Elisha used to cook breakfast for me while I drank coffee and read the morning paper. The smell of breakfast cooking and the backside of a woman working in the kitchen must have triggered something in my brain.

Rachel brought my plate and saw me wiping tears from my eyes with the back of my hand.

"That'll happen for awhile," she said. "After a concussion it's common to have trouble controlling your emotions. Anger's the worst, sometimes you just go off for no reason." Rachel gave me a lingering grin, "It's like having PMS."

Elisha got PMS something awful. Whenever she craved chocolate, I tiptoed around her.

My eggs were scrambled, a little runny for my liking, but the bacon was perfect and I wasn't about to complain.

Rachel was eating buttered toast and sipping orange juice from an empty peanut butter jar. "If you hold that down," she said. "I'll give you something that'll make you feel better."

I could use something to make me feel better. Overwhelming grief turned into unbridled feelings of guilt. I had killed Elisha. I didn't cut her heart out with a knife like I did in my dreams. What I did was worse. When she found out about the affair, she gave up and let the leukemia take her. Tears ran down my cheeks and I left the table to wash my face in the bathroom.

Cold water helped a little. Elisha filed for divorce, not wanting me near her while she was dying. But the worst part for me to accept was that I was actually relieved when she finally died. The illness had been long and she suffered constantly. All day, every day, I was tortured by what I'd done to her. When Elisha finally died, I didn't have to face her anymore. I had killed her and then was relieved when she was gone. It was a horrible way to feel and I couldn't forgive myself for that. Not ever. I still loved her desperately.

"I can reheat your breakfast," Rachel said when I came back from the bathroom.

"It's fine."

Rachel watched me eat while I tried not to cry. "Would you like me to get your mind off whatever you're thinking about?" she asked.

"How are you going to do that?"

"By talking about something else," she said. "We had a very interesting night last night. I want to run a couple of things by you."

"Interesting?" I asked. "How so?"

"To begin with," she said, leaning forward, elbows on the table, swirling orange juice in the old peanut jar. "Fat Louie is dead."

"Dead?"

"Graveyard dead." Rachel stood up, fetched the coffee pot and topped off my kitty cup. "I'll be right back."

When she returned, she held three pills in the palm of her hand. "This will make you feel better, it's a little something I learned in Iraq. We dealt with quite a few head trauma cases. You shouldn't take them on an empty stomach."

She emptied her palm into mine. There was a small blue pill, an oval yellow pill, and a thick round white pill. She poured me some more orange juice to wash the pills down with.

"What is this stuff?" I asked.

"Don't worry, the military has tested it in combat. You'll feel better."

Since I didn't think I could feel any worse, I washed the pills down with one gulp.

"Tell me about Fat Louie," I said.

Rachel sat at the table, toyed with her orange juice and took a moment to start talking.

"It wasn't pretty. He was a scumbag, but nobody should die like that."

"What do you mean?"

"They tortured him."

"How?"

"Beating, knife cuts, needles under the fingernails, electric shock to his testicles, and I mean they used straight electricity from an extension cord, not 12-volt batteries." She shook her head. "It was brutal. He was tied up and had his pants down around his ankles. The guy shit and pissed all over himself before he died."

"How'd you find him?"

"The bartender from next door called it in. He was taking trash out to the alley and heard Fat Louie screaming. By the time we responded, whoever did it had cleared out and Fat Louie was dead. The bartender gave us a partial license number and a description of the vehicle he saw parked in the alley. We may get lucky."

"Was it robbery or revenge?"

"The safe wasn't open and it didn't look like a typical robbery, we see a lot of those and this was different. No, I'm guessing that somebody had a grudge to settle or wanted information and Fat Louie wasn't giving it to them."

"He should have just given them what they wanted."

"Maybe they were asking him questions he didn't know the answers to."

"If he died an ugly death, maybe it was revenge for the kiddie porn he was into."

"I don't think so, he wasn't into that end of it. He was only a collector, not a perpetrator, and besides, the box of porn was still there, they were after something else."

By now the pills were dissolving in my stomach and the faint tingling in my lips and toes told me the drugs were entering my bloodstream. I took another sip of orange juice and found that the metallic taste was fading. "What did you give me?"

"Is it working?"

"Like a charm."

"It was a little pharmaceutical cocktail of pain killer, anti-inflammatory, and mild stimulant."

"You're dealing drugs now?"

"Personal use. And I'll deny I ever gave it to you, I'll say you got into my medicine cabinet."

Rachel's cell phone rang and she took the call in her bedroom. The kitty cup was getting low so I got more coffee and stood at the sliding glass door looking out at the beach. Joggers were interfering with the bird's work at the surf line.

"James Wierman died of blunt force trauma to the head," she said when she came back. "He'd been beaten before he died."

Rachel sat at the table and I followed her cue.

"Wierman had several things in his pocket, a set of keys to the ship, a pocket knife, and some change. His car keys weren't on him," she said. "The forensics people couldn't pull prints from the entire ship, but they did check the chief engineer's office and bedroom."

The pills were really kicking in now and the pain in my head was nothing more than a dull ache.

"Here's the thing that's interesting," she said, leaning forward on the table, resting on her elbows. "One set of prints we pulled came back as classified."

"Classified?"

"Yes, and about two minutes after we ran them, we got a phone call from Langley and they wanted to know why we were running those prints."

"CIA? What did you tell them?"

"My Lieutenant did the talking. They wanted to know where we found the prints and under what circumstances. After he told them, they just hung up on him."

Rachel was deep in thought. "Something about that ship keeps getting people killed. First the guard in Suisun Bay, then Wierman, they left you for dead, and now Fat Louie."

"You think Fat Louie got killed because of the *Balboa Victory*?" Suddenly I was glad I only got hit in the head instead of having a live electrical cord held to my testicles. Just the thought of it made me grimace.

"I'm trying to add it all up," she said. "First, Wierman is beaten and killed, then his house burglarized, and when his daughter gives you a letter he wrote, somebody smacks you in the head and steals it. Think about it, if you got rolled by a couple of crackhead punks looking for drug money, they wouldn't have taken the letter from your car. We're pretty damn sure Fat Louie was fencing items stolen from the ship, so I can't help but think he was holding out on us yesterday and had something else, something that got him killed."

"Didn't the guy that found Wierman's body the other night say something about three seamen getting killed in the cargo hold years ago?"

"I forgot about that," she said.

Rachel lapsed deep into thought again and I could see the wheels turning in her mind.

"There's one more thing that doesn't add up," she said after a moment. "You being a sailor and all, maybe you would know."

"What's that?"

"Wierman had a pocket knife on him," she said. "The crime lab found traces of silver paint and gold on it along with grease and manila rope fibers."

"Silver paint and gold paint?"

"No. Silver paint and traces of real, pure, gold."

"Gold?"

"Yeah, where would you find that combination on a ship?"

The scarce knowledge I'd gleaned from all the marine engineering classes at the Coast Guard Academy years ago was stowed in darkest recesses of my mind, but I didn't recall anything aboard ship using gold. Maybe some wiring for high-end electronics would contain gold, but I doubted it, and certainly the *Balboa Victory* wasn't equipped with expensive electronic gear. Why the silver paint?

"I can't think of anything, but I have some engineer friends that might know," I said.

Rachel finished her orange juice and then rinsed the peanut butter jar in the sink. "I'm going to take a shower and then I'll run you over to your place to get a few things. You should probably stay here until you feel better and we figure out what's going on."

I looked into my coffee cup and briefly considered not asking my question. "What's with the suitcases?" I blurted, not able to suppress the sudden impulse. "Are you going someplace?"

Rachel turned sullen. "What? Are you snooping now?"

"I tripped over them in the middle of the night and damn near broke my neck. I was just wondering."

She walked out of the kitchen and into the living room without saying anything. Just when I was convinced she was going to ignore the question, she turned around.

"It helps me get by," she said, her eyes narrow and jaw firm, hands twitching at her thighs. "I know that if I can't stand the bullshit anymore, I can be packed in ten minutes and be on a bus or airplane out of town."

She stared at me, waiting for a response, her eyes challenging me to say something. The look in her face was familiar, it was the same expression she wore when she'd questioned Fat Louie at the pawnshop yesterday. I had a few more things I was curious about, but I sure as shit wasn't going to ask any more questions right now.

13

Other than occasionally cursing at cars that didn't move fast enough for her when a traffic light turned green, Rachel was quiet while she drove me back to my place. I wasn't sure if it was because she was tired from working all night or because I'd asked her about the suitcases. It could be a combination of the two. Then again, maybe it was something all together different.

"I was just thinking," I said to break the silence. "Whoever killed Fat Louie may be looking for that Canetti kid if all this has to do with the *Balboa Victory*."

"We're professionals," Rachel said, her demeanor still brusque. "We've already thought of that and the day shift is handling it."

My temper flared because of the tone she'd used with me. I started to say something but managed to bite my tongue. It's just the PMS I told myself and tried to relax.

Bill Baldwin, the manager of the Bonita Apartments, was a barrel-chested bald man in his sixties with gray tufts of hair over his ears and a mouth full of bad teeth. We found him in his ground-floor office and he had a spare key for me to go along with a string of apologies and feeble explanations that he offered up like cheap hors d'oeuvres served at a two-bit gin mill during happy hour.

"We've never had anything like this happen before," he said, leaning in a little too close, exhaling day-old coffee breath on me. "I'm going to change the locks on that door for you. No charge, it's on us."

"Thanks," I said.

"I'm doing that today and I'll have new keys for you this afternoon," he added, standing outside the office door to leer at Rachel as we walked away.

There was a piece of white paper taped to my apartment door. It was a note from Julio Reynoza saying that he had my groceries. The note also said that he hoped I was doing okay and was sorry he hadn't confronted the guy he's seen sitting in my car. Julio's note explained that he didn't know anything was wrong until he found me by the elevator and by then the guy was gone.

As I stuck the key in the door lock, Rachel brushed past me and closely inspected the door. Using a fingernail, she removed a thin piece of clear tape at the top of the door.

"Nobody's been inside," she said, showing me the unbroken piece of tape and explaining how she'd put it there to see if anybody entered the apartment later last night using my keys. "They must have taken what they needed from you."

I half expected the place to be trashed or torn apart anyway but was pleasantly surprised to discover that wasn't the case. Since Rachel had never been to my apartment, she nosed around a little while I took a quick shower and dressed. There weren't any clean Coast Guard uniforms in my closet so I picked out a pair of gray slacks, a red tie to go with a white dress shirt, and a dark blue jacket. In the kitchen, Rachel helped me get the gauze unstuck from my head and wipe the blood from my hair because I hadn't done it in the shower. The cut on my head was still oozing.

After collecting all my dirty uniforms that needed to go the dry cleaners, Rachel and I took the elevator to the garage to see where I had been attacked.

The spot in front of the elevator where I'd been assaulted the previous night had been cleaned up, and other than an occasional whiff of bleach and Lysol, you would never know that anything violent happened there.

"I need permission to have your government car towed to the crime lab," Rachel said. "It'll be interesting to see what we find."

"Sure," I said. "I don't have keys to it anyway, I'll need to get another car from the motor pool."

That's when it happened, like getting struck with a bolt of lightning. My shrink had been speaking enough psychobabble to me that the tiny rational part of my brain knew it was really nothing more than a simple case of sublimation. The complications due to the concussion and the side effects of the pills Rachel gave me probably didn't help, but standing where I'd been attacked, intense anger grew inside of me, and that anger suddenly flashed into unmanageable rage. The bevy of latent emotions I still had for Elisha and the devastation of her lingering death, the lifelong tumultuous relationships with my brothers and dead father, and the bitter disappointment I felt for everything that had gone wrong I my life was unleashed and then all came together, funneled into to one simple and pure thought that I could do something about. Revenge. I would hunt down the assholes that had done this to me and make them pay. Avenging the deaths of James Wierman and Fat Louie would be icing on the cake.

"Are you okay?" Rachel asked, her tired brown eyes full of concern.

"I'm fine. Now."

After doubling back to my apartment to get a spare bottle of my happy pills from the bathroom to replace the one I'd lost last night somewhere along the way, Rachel took me to drop off my dry cleaning and then to work. Traffic was moving at a crawl as we headed across the Vincent Thomas Bridge toward Terminal Island and from the passenger seat of her car, I had a clear view of both the *Dixie Victory* and her sister ship, the *Balboa Victory*, berthed one ahead of the other along the main shipping channel. Rachel was quiet again while she drove so I worked on containing my emotions by developing a plan to flush out my attackers. So far, I knew I'd need bait and a trap. I just wasn't sure of the details yet. I was thinking more of what I'd do to them when I found them.

We couldn't get on the Coast Guard Base because I didn't have any identification and Rachel had two shotguns and body armor in her trunk, not to mention that hog-leg she carries on her left hip. I explained to the rosy-cheeked sentry that the standing orders posted in the guardhouse were signed by me, but since he was fairly new to the base and didn't know me by sight yet, Yeoman Jenkins had to be summoned to the front gate so I could get signed in.

Rachel slammed her trunk lid and stood next to me, pressing a small plastic baggie into my hand. "Try not to take these more than every six hours," she said. "I have to work tonight so you're welcome to stay at my place again."

I squeezed her hand before slipping the baggie into my pocket. "Thanks, I may do that."

It took about an hour to fill out the paperwork for a new military identification card and to explain to the female Ensign in charge of the motor pool why the vehicle she'd assigned me less than two months earlier had been impounded by the San Pedro Police Department, and for that reason, I needed her to let me have another one. She winced when I showed her my scalp, and after I signed several other lengthy government forms, she forked over the keys to another generic government low-bid sedan.

Once back in my office, I called and cancelled the two credit cards that had been in my wallet, informed the bank that I'd need a new card to access their cash machines, and made an appointment with California Department of Motor Vehicles to get another driver's license. By ten-thirty on Thursday morning, I'd shuffled thru the day's paperwork, setting the lower priority things to the side to be handled later, and completely cleared my schedule for the rest of the day so I could concentrate on the Wierman case.

Pressing my fingers to my scalp, I ruminated about my options and where I should start first. The blood on my fingers was fresh and I wiped it off with a tissue. Probably should have just got the damn stitches last night. At the moment, I wasn't sure why I'd put up such a fight.

James Wierman's Merchant Marine service record would be a good place to start. Every time a merchant seaman serves aboard a vessel, his sea time is recorded by that vessel's master and reported to the Coast Guard via a certificate known as a discharge. The discharge contains pertinent information about the vessel and the dates and places the seaman signed on and off. A lazy voiced clerk in the basement of the Coast Guard archives building back in Washington told me it would take four to six weeks for him the get me the information I needed because all discharges had been placed on microfiche and there was a waiting list. After reiterating to him the importance of the information I needed for an active murder investigation, he again told me it would take from four to six weeks. PMS can be a useful tool if used properly. I explained to the lazy-voiced clerk on the other end of the phone, in no uncertain terms, that if the information I needed wasn't on my desk by the end of the workday, he would find himself transferred to a Coast Guard fisheries surveillance vessel based in Alaska's Aleutian Islands. Apparently, he'd already heard the horror stories about that assignment and figured maybe I had the horsepower to pull off my threat because he suddenly changed his tone, assuring me that my request would not be a problem.

Tracking down the report of the three seamen killed on the *Balboa Victory* in 1970 proved easier because the information had been entered on our central database. According to the Coast Guard investigation of the incident at the time, the cause was improper stowage of military ordnance bound for Vietnam that had been loaded at a facility near Seattle. The report stated that the stevedore company used by the government was cutting corners to save money on a fixed bid contract and as a result, inferior and insufficient shoring materials were used to keep the bombs from shifting when the ship was at sea. When the *Balboa Victory* hit rough weather four days out of port in the North Pacific, some of the bombs broke loose in #3 cargo hold and the ship's crew was mustered to re-secure them. Witnesses said lights had been rigged in the cargo hold and work was underway to neutralize the movement of several thousand-pound bombs when a severe roll caused other bombs to shift, crushing three crewmembers before they had a chance to get out of the way. The report went on to say that another ship, the *S.S. Badger State,* loaded bombs at the same port after the *Balboa Victory* and when their cargo shifted, the entire ship was lost with a mere twelve crewmembers surviving the sinking by taking to the lifeboats in storm tossed seas.

How did three merchant seamen being crushed by bombs in the cargo hold of the *Balboa Victory* on its way to Vietnam in 1970 have anything to do with James Wierman getting killed two days ago and me getting roughed-up last night? Frank Burch, the chief engineer on the *Dixie Victory* who found Wierman's body the other night, had said the *Balboa Victory* was haunted. What did he mean by that? And what did the FBI know about that security guard that was killed while the ship was still laid-up in Suisun Bay? Now, to top it all off, Fat Louie, a low life pawnshop owner that was fencing marine collectibles that were probably stolen from the ship, was dead as well. How did this all tie together?

Yeoman Jenkins came into my office with a fax from Malcolm Cross. The two-page fax listed the Cabrillo Vo-Tech students and the hours each worked aboard the *Balboa Victory*. However, it didn't give details about which student worked which days or what their work assignments were. There were forty-one students listed, some worked as little as four total hours while some had over a hundred hours. The list was useless to me. I needed to know who had worked with James Wierman before he died and what they did. Now, I would have to interview each of the forty-one students listed and the fax didn't even give their contact phone numbers. It looked like I needed to pay another visit to Mr. Malcolm Cross.

I checked my watch, couldn't remember when I'd taken my first set of pills at Rachel's apartment, said what the hell to myself, opened the baggie, and chased one more of each color down with coffee.

James Wierman's pocketknife had me puzzled. Rachel said it had traces of grease, manila fibers, silver paint and gold. The grease was easy. It was everywhere in the engine room. Manila fibers would be from manila rope that was a common as rust on a ship. James Wierman had obviously cut a piece of rope with the knife at some point in time. Silver paint, more specifically, aluminized silver paint, was often used to coat steam lines in the engine room. Again, not unusual. But why would he have traces of gold on his knife?

Dan Burns would know if there was a reason for a chief engineer to have gold on his pocketknife. Dan Burns and I had gone to the Coast Guard Academy together and he'd spent a lot of time in our Marine Inspection division after graduation. He had a lot of shipyard time under his belt working with new construction as well as the annual equipment and safety inspections we did on U.S. flagged merchant ships. Somewhere along the line he'd been promoted to Captain and was now stationed back in Washington as the Coast Guard's officer-in-charge of the Marine Safety Office. We rarely spoke these days, being assigned to different offices, but we'd been teammates on the Academy rowing team and crewed in the same eight-man boat for three years. It didn't matter how much time had passed since our last phone conversation. We'd be friends forever.

Elisha and I first met at the fall regatta while I was in the Coast Guard Academy. Unlike football games with their traditional tailgate fare consisting of beer and hotdogs, rowing regattas are quite the cultured event. Rows of neatly painted wooden armchairs were set up on the magnificent lawns overlooking the finish line on the Thames River in New London, Connecticut. Men dressed in blazers and ties with their school pins displayed on the lapel chatted with women in long flowery dresses and sun hats. Regattas are catered and white-jacketed waiters served the outdoor buffet line from silver covered trays of haute cuisine. Hot dogs and hamburgers at a regatta would be heresy.

It was after the race, when everyone gathered to dine and await the presentation of the trophies, that I bumped into Elisha and spilled her drink. She told me that she was attending the regatta because her brother rowed for Massachusetts Institute of Technology team and she'd come up with her family from Virginia where they had a home not far from Tappahannock. She introduced me to her father; a senior executive for one of Virginia's elite defense industry contractors. I didn't know at the time she was only in high school. Since she was drinking alcohol, I assumed she was of age, and it wasn't until months later when she asked me if I would escort her to her senior prom in my Coast Guard dress-whites, that I discovered her true age. Years later, in an intimate moment, she confessed that she'd orchestrated the encounter with the spilled drink because she was so taken by the handsome oarsman in his Coast Guard Midshipman uniform.

"Are you still rowing?" asked Dan Burns after he finally came on the line.

"Whenever I can, I keep my scull in the fire department boathouse. How about you?"

"I try to get out every weekend, we have a rowing club here on the Potomac. You should come by the next time you're out this way."

Dan Burns listened patiently while I babbled on about James Wierman's murder, the FBI and CIA being at the murder scene, Wierman's house getting burglarized, the contents of the letter his daughter gave me, how I'd been hit from behind and the letter stolen, Fat Louie's brutal murder, and the gold found on James Wierman's knife.

"You've got your hands full out there," Dan Burns said. "But it sounds right on the money about how the *SeaTrans Expeditor* was lost. I don't personally know about the Navy intentionally scuttling ships during the Vietnam War, but I do know that during World War Two, the crews of merchant ships were told to sink their vessels instead of letting both it and the war materials fall into enemy hands where they could be used against us. All the ships built during that era were specifically designed for scuttling in a matter of minutes."

"How about the gold?" I asked. "Would the chief engineer of an old Victory ship be scraping anything made of gold?"

"Not on that ship, there's nothing made of gold on those old rust buckets. They were built of steel, brass, bronze, and had wooden hatch covers, but no gold anywhere. Did you ever think that that he may have picked up the traces of gold someplace else?"

"That's always a possibility," I said, suddenly thinking about the jewelry Brooke Wierman was wearing. But would she let her father work on her jewelry with a pocketknife? Probably not.

"I'll tell you what I'll do," Dan Burns said. "We'll have a copy of the *SeaTrans Expeditor's* casualty report in our office. I'll look it over for you, let you know what I think, and then do a little digging to see if any of the old crewmembers are still around to talk to, but I have to warn you, that was a long time ago and most of those guys are probably dead by now."

Dan Burns and I talked about rowing for a few more minutes and I promised him I'd stop by next time I was in town so we could take a boat out on the Potomac for old times sake.

Sitting at my desk and doing a little math, I figured that Admiral Greenwalt, the Navy officer that asked James Wierman to scuttle the SeaTrans Expeditor in the first place, might still be alive. Hopefully, he'd taken care of himself and was living in some sunny retirement community where he played golf every day and bored his friends with his sea stories.

Being a Coast Guard Commander didn't open many doors for me at the Bureau of Naval Personnel. I got the typical bureaucratic runaround. I told my story countless times only to be put on hold. It was starting to look like I was doing nothing more than chasing my own tail when Commander Stillwell came on the line.

"What can I do for you, Commander Stanton?" he asked.

I spilled my story about the active murder investigation and James Wierman's letter one more time, explaining I would like to know if Admiral Greenwalt was still alive, and if so, where I could contact him.

"Hold on, Commander."

It was about ten minutes before Commander Stillwell came back on the line. "Commander Stanton?"

"I'm still here."

"Normally, Commander, you would need to go through proper channels to access the information you need, and quite frankly, that's a long and frustrating process."

"I work for the government, too."

"I'm aware of that, Commander. But under the circumstances, I feel I can disburse some information."

"Great."

"Not great," Commander Stillwell said. "The Navy didn't have an Admiral named Greenwalt on staff at any time during the Vietnam War."

14

Yeoman Jenkins must have heard my coffee cup hit the wall and the string of profanities coming from inside my office, because when he came through the door, he was bug-eyed and pale.

"Is everything...?" he asked, quickly looking around my office, appearing surprised to find me alone. "Can I get you anything, Commander?"

"A shotgun and one shell."

"Pardon me, sir?"

"Never mind. I'm fine, there's a situation, that's all."

"If you need anything..." he said, easing the door closed.

It was obvious that I needed to get a grip on myself. A little frustration shouldn't cause me to fly off the handle. It's just that I wanted to find out what the hell was really going on with the *Balboa Victory* and get my hands on the dirty rotten chicken-fuckers that cheap-shotted me in my garage so I could exact my revenge. I wasn't going to feel better about anything until that happened.

Once I had a moment to think about it, the whole thing made perfect sense. Why would Admiral Greenwalt use his real name? If he really were conducting a top-secret operation during wartime, he wouldn't be out of line to use another name. I'd used several aliases when I was undercover in Boca Raton. Hell, married men use fake names all the time when they hit on women in bars.

Then again, maybe none of the pieces to the puzzle were related at all. Maybe I was trying to put together a series of random events. Maybe James Wierman got in a fight with the chief engineer on the *Dixie Victory* over some spare parts, took a couple of punches and went down, accidentally hitting his head. Old guys get grumpy. But that would be manslaughter at best, not murder. Maybe the burglary at Wierman's house had something to do with whoever was looting the ships. Wierman might have taken a few very valuable things home for safekeeping, the looters wanted to get their hands on the items so they could pawn them, and so they hit his house when they knew he was gone. Maybe the letter Brooke Wierman gave me didn't have anything to do with me getting mugged. Maybe I'd been worked over by a couple of punks looking to steal my wallet and car but Julio scared them off before they finished. There were certainly plenty of gangs and piddling punks roaming the streets of San Pedro these days. And maybe the only reason somebody did Fat Louie the way they did is because he deserved it. He damn sure wasn't a saint. As for the gold, maybe James Wierman was painting steam lines in the engineroom, got some paint on his wedding band, and then scraped it off. That would explain the traces of gold on his pocketknife. But then again, that's a lot of maybes.

The only thing that didn't have a 'maybe' attached to it was the fact that agents from both the FBI and CIA showed up at the crime scene without being called. And it still didn't make sense to me why the CIA wanted James Wierman's body.

It was twelve-thirty and I was getting hungry. It occurred to me that maybe I should just go to lunch and forget about the whole damn thing. I could take a few days off in order to get my emotions under control and let the cut on my head heal. Repressing my feelings and taking happy pills was working just fine before somebody cracked my skull open.

But no matter how hard I tried to think about something else and do other work, I just couldn't let it go. It was like an itch I had to scratch. You know scratching it is only going to make it worse, but you can't help doing it anyway. The Wierman case was under my skin and driving me nuts.

Lloyd Waller had been at the crime scene on the *Balboa Victory* for the FBI and I debated on whether or not to call him. He'd been evasive the other night and I had no reason to believe he'd be forthcoming with me now. His business card had been in my wallet and so it took me about fifteen minutes of navigating the bureaucratic maze known as the FBI's San Pedro Field Office before I could get somebody to give me his cell phone number.

Lloyd Waller and I chatted for a few minutes and without giving away too many details, I hit the highlights of what happened at Wierman's house, Fat Louie turning up dead after fencing items stolen from the ship, and how I'd been mugged and lost the letter James Wierman wrote confessing he intentionally sank the *SeaTrans Expeditor*. Sometimes less is more.

"It kind of makes me wonder what you're not telling me about this case, Lloyd."

"I'm not sure what you mean."

"I know about the gold."

There was a slight pause before he responded and I knew immediately that I'd hit pay dirt. You can't bullshit a bullshitter.

"What gold?" he said.

"Come on, Lloyd, don't try to feed me that crap," I said. It was too late for him, he'd fumbled the ball and I was going to pick it up and run with it. "Here's how I look at it, Lloyd. I know just enough about what's going on here to really screw it up, and I'm pissed off enough about getting the shit kicked out of me that there's no way I'm going to back off. I'm going to keep digging around, asking questions, and the whole damn thing is going to snowball out of control for the Bureau. You know me, I'll eventually find out what's going on, and by then, a lot of people are going to be up to their eyeballs in shit and..."

"Okay."

"Okay what?"

"We'll meet."

"Where are you?"

"In the field."

"Have you had lunch?"

"No."

"How long will it take you to get to San Pedro?"

Lloyd paused. "About thirty minutes."

"Harbor Light, thirty minutes. Do you know it?"

"Sure."

"And, Lloyd," I said.

"What?"

"You're buying, they stole my wallet."

***

It was twenty minutes past one when I parked my newly acquired government sedan on 4th street in San Pedro. The sun had emerged and the sky overhead was brilliant blue, but closer to the ground, fog lingered, and a pale rainbow streamed from horizon to horizon in the south like a huge arch that had been painted with watercolors and then just hung in the sky from a nail. I waited for a break in traffic and then jogged across the street, the bouncing motion making my head wound throb.

Reverend Johnny and another vagrant were working the lunch crowd on the sidewalk outside the Harbor Light. Johnny wore his usual tattered fatigues, combat boots, and headphones. He sat on the sidewalk, knees drawn to his chest, and next to him were his boom box and a large cardboard sign that proclaimed 'JESUS IS THE

WAY, THE TRUTH, AND THE LIGHT' in six-inch tall block letters. Johnny's partner, a ruddy sort with long hair and a scraggly beard, wore Salvation Army rejects and a large hat that made him look like the scarecrow in the Wizard of Oz.

Beverly Cristy said she thought Reverend Johnny was a fake so I gave him a closer look today. I've seen my share of fakes and con men, but Johnny sure looked like a socially dysfunctional byproduct of war to me. Vietnam Vets had replaced the World War Two and Korean War Vets on the sidewalks, and now the Vietnam bunch was slowly dying off, only to have their spots taken by a steady stream of combat-damaged men that faithfully served our country in Afghanistan and Iraq.

I reached for my wallet to drop a couple of bucks in their coffee can, but came up empty. "I'll have to catch you another time," I explained to Johnny's partner. "I lost my wallet yesterday."

"Whatever is, has already been," Reverend Johnny said as I stepped past him. "And what will be has been before, and God will call the past into account."

Lloyd Waller was in the bar and sitting in my seat when I got there. Although the restaurant side was busy, we had the bar to ourselves. Doris, the daytime bartender, was probably the main reason Lloyd and I were her only customers. She was a beefy woman in her mid-thirties with hostile eyes and kinky brown hair she wore short. She made no bones about hating men and if I hadn't seen her boyfriend, a greasy tattooed biker dude that came in one day and verbally abused her until she gave him money from her purse, I'd swear she was a bull dyke.

We both ordered ice tea and Doris rolled her eyes.

"I'll have a bacon cheeseburger with fries," Lloyd said, folding his menu and handing it back to Doris.

"Make it two," I said without looking at a menu.

Doris ducked under the bar to place our orders in the kitchen.

"Tell me what you know about the gold," Lloyd said.

"We're not playing that game." I said. The only thing I had going for me was a hunch and a bluff, so I needed to play this for all it was worth. "I told you I only know enough to screw things up and there's a lot you're not telling me. It's time for you to come clean. People are getting killed over this, and I came damn close to being one of them. I obviously know quite a bit, or they wouldn't have busted my melon and left me for dead."

Lloyd was silent while he studied his fingernails. "You did know that SeaTrans was operated by the CIA during the Vietnam War didn't you?" he said when he finally spoke. "Sort of like the maritime version of Air America."

Doris brought the ice tea and then returned to her perch at the far end of the bar.

"That fits," I said. Maybe that's why the Navy wouldn't acknowledge they had an Admiral Greenwalt.

Lloyd lowered his voice and leaned toward me. "They needed a way to move heavy items that couldn't be flown from stateside and they weren't all too happy with involving the military in their sneaky little schemes, so they set up their own shipping company."

"I see."

"Anyway, Franklin Sheridan was put in charge of SeaTrans, his background was in Naval Intelligence and being an Annapolis graduate, he knew something about ships so he was perfect for the job. They pulled a few strings back in Washington and got a few old Victory ships from the Maritime Administration out of the layup fleets around the country, rented some office space here in San Pedro, and went to work shipping legitimate military cargo, occasionally mixing in something special they needed and nobody was the wiser."

"What does this have to do with the gold?"

"Are you familiar with Bretton Woods?"

"Doesn't ring a bell."

"It was a conference during World War Two, where the allies got together at a place called Bretton Woods, and agreed on how the postwar currencies would be based on gold at an agreed set value. The purpose was to prevent rampant speculation and inflation after the war."

"I'm not much of an economist."

"One of the provisions of Bretton Woods was that if one country accumulated enough currency from another country, they could ask for payment in gold."

"So?"

"By 1971, the United States was experiencing a huge trade deficit and our currency, based on the gold standard, was failing. President Nixon eventually abandoned it in favor of the flat currency we use now, but I won't go into that. According to Bretton Woods, gold was given a set value of thirty-five dollars an ounce, but in 1971 it was worth much more than that on the world black market. We owed a lot of countries money because of the huge bills we were running up during the Vietnam War and they were asking to be paid in gold. The CIA knew that they could get more bang for their buck if they used gold, so they were transporting gold to Vietnam to fund their shady back-water operations."

"So the CIA was shipping gold overseas on SeaTrans ships?"

"Right. One shipment of a million and a half ounces, that's just under fifty tons, was supposed to have been on the *SeaTrans Expeditor* when she went to the bottom of the South China Sea."

"Supposed to have been?"

"That's right. The gold was loaded on the *SeaTrans Expeditor* at one point, and our theory is that somebody took the gold off and then sent the ship to the bottom of the ocean to cover up the crime."

"Shit!" I said, doing the math in my head to find out how much the gold was worth. One and a half million ounces at thirty-five dollars an ounce would be about fifty million dollars. Of course at today's prices, the same gold would be worth well over a billion. No wonder people were getting killed.

"By the time the Bureau got involved, the trail was cold. They put about thirty agents on it and they figured the switch, if it actually took place, happened in the Philippines. One of the ships in the Philippines at the same time as the *SeaTrans Expeditor* was the *Balboa Victory,* again, operated by SeaTrans. The Bureau tore the ship apart once it got back stateside but they never found any trace of the gold, and like I said, by the time the Bureau was called in, the trail had gone cold anyway. The CIA had egg all over its face and didn't want anybody to know what happened so they weren't cooperating much and the whole incident was quietly swept under the bureaucratic carpet."

"James Wierman had a pocketknife on him when he died," I said. "It had traces of silver paint and gold on it."

Lloyd Waller sipped his iced tea and nodded. "I heard that."

"So what made the CIA think somebody snatched their gold instead of it accidentally going to the bottom of the ocean, which by the way, we now know for sure wasn't the case."

"They had their suspicions, things they heard here and there."

"Anybody in particular?"

"Somebody by the name of Bailey, a Captain with Naval Intelligence that was working with the Navy SEALS in Vietnam. Once the gold got in-country, the CIA was using the Navy SEALS to move it around where they needed it."

"Why the SEALS?"

"They were a new and elite combat unit at that time. Nobody knew much about them back then, or what they did over there. All the Agency guys in Vietnam stuck out like Japanese tourists on Coney Island and the SEALS moved wherever they wanted, whenever they wanted, and since they were a real kick-ass outfit, nobody fucked with them."

"Did they confront this Bailey character?"

"They couldn't. Bailey and six SEALS went missing-in-action in the Mekong Delta about the time the gold disappeared. They weren't anywhere near the gold, the gold was on a ship in the South China Sea and Bailey and his boys were confirmed in combat in some rice paddy."

"But the Bureau suspected James Wierman was involved."

Lloyd looked at me funny. "How do you know?"

"It was in his letter somebody took from me last night."

"I've been looking over the old reports and the Bureau was looking really hard at the captain and the chief engineer of the *SeaTrans Expeditor*. The Bureau followed them for years, checking their finances and movements."

"What did they turn up?"

"Nothing. Over time, the agents doing the investigation concluded that neither one had anything to do with the gold." Lloyd Waller sipped his tea. "Until now, that is."

"How about Franklin Sheridan?" I asked. "He took SeaTrans from a small company in the

1960's to the mega-corporation it is today. The man's got a ton of money."

"The Bureau watched him like a hawk, but he never went near any gold, at least not that we knew of. His business expansion and finances were all legitimate. After Vietnam, the CIA ended their association with both Sheridan and SeaTrans. I guess there was bad blood between them over the missing gold.

Doris brought our burgers and served them with a bottle of ketchup, a jar of brown mustard, and a scowl.

We were both hungry and dug into our food without talking. When we finished, Lloyd Waller reached for his wallet.

"I hate to eat and run, but I have other things to do," he said. "We're good. Right?"

"What do you mean?"

"You're going to stop looking into this now, right?" Lloyd Waller said. "I told you what I know about the gold, that was the deal."

"I'll stop looking into it when I find the shit-birds that split my head open. That was completely uncalled for. If they wanted the letter, hell, I'd have made them a photocopy."

"Let us handle it from here, Jared. I've already told you more than I should have."

Lloyd stood up to leave.

"I have one more question," I said.

"What's that?"

"You said that both Franklin Sheridan and this Bailey guy that went missing-in-action were both with Naval Intelligence," I said. "Did they know each other?"

Lloyd Waller put his hand on my shoulder. "Jared, you've got a concussion, let us handle this thing, okay?" he said. "Take a few days off. Get some rest. You really need to let this go, I'd hate to see anything else happen to you."

15

Both the rainbow and Reverend Johnny had vanished by the time I left the Harbor Light. Traffic on 4th Street was sparse because everyone had gone back to work for the afternoon, so I jaywalked back to my car. It was just past two and I sat in the government sedan, contemplating my next move.

Originally, I'd planned on stopping by the SeaTrans office to confront Malcolm Cross about the fax he'd sent me this morning, but given what I'd just learned from Lloyd Waller, it seemed pretty remote that a Cabrillo Vo-Tech student had anything to do with James Wierman's death. Besides, Lloyd Waller had warned me off the case and because of my status with Homeland Security, I'd have to be a little more discreet about my involvement from now on.

My apartment was only five minutes away and I decided to drop by to find out if the manager had my new keys yet. Opening the security gate to the underground garage at the Bonita

Apartments required a remote control, and since mine had either been stolen last night or towed to the SPPD impound lot with my other car this morning, I parked out front on the street.

Bill Baldwin wasn't in his office, but hanging on the door was one of those fake clocks with adjustable hands showing what time he expected to return. The hands on the clock were set for 1:00 PM, but he was over an hour late. I took the stairs to the third floor and as soon as I left the stairwell, I could see someone fooling with the lock on my apartment door. Logic told me it was the locksmith the manager arranged. Paranoia told me it was somebody else.

There was the usual commotion blaring from inside the Reynoza brother's apartment and when I knocked on their door, the guy working on my apartment door lock looked up without speaking. I knocked again, louder this time, and when nobody answered, I walked down the hall toward my apartment.

"I live here," I said to the guy kneeling on the floor.

"I'll be done in a few minutes," he said. "Do you need to get in?"

"Sure."

The guy stood up to let me pass. He was wearing dark blue pants and a light blue work shirt that had an embroidered patch advertising 'San Pedro Lockworks' sewn above the right pocket. The name 'Gary' was embroidered over the left pocket. His tools were in a brown leather pouch on the floor.

"You must do a lot of this," I said.

"All the time." He kneeled down to continue his work.

My apartment looked the same as I'd left it a few hours earlier. Without warning, an overwhelming feeling of paranoia consumed me. It was the same feeling millions of crime victims feel each year, an unconscious conversion of instinctual impulses as a result of being violated. Paranoia, fear, anger, helplessness, and sorrow are fused into a single irrational emotion that is almost impossible to deal with. Fortunately, I've got a bottle of little white pills to take care of that.

This wasn't the first time I'd experienced an emotion like this. Soon after Elisha and I were married, our Miami Beach apartment was burglarized while we were at the movies. We didn't lose much, we were newly married and poor since I was only getting Coast Guard Ensign pay, but what little we had, was scattered everywhere. Elisha refused to spend the night in the apartment after the police left and I was forced to book a hotel room for us. Even though the locks were changed, Elisha insisted we move to a safer neighborhood where she promptly installed multiple chains on the doors of the new apartment. My response to the incident wasn't as pronounced as Elisha's, but I certainly knew what she had gone through.

I glanced back at the locksmith, ran water in the kitchen sink until it was cold, and then washed one of my happy pills down with a glass of tap water. Two days after our Miami Beach burglary, Elisha clipped an article from the Miami Herald about a serial rapist in Georgia that gained access to his victim's apartments by keeping copies of their keys when he changed their locks. My frequent absences because of work were probably a contributing factor, but Elisha never felt completely safe in her own home again.

"I'm done." Gary stepped inside my apartment and displayed some keys. "Two for you and two for the manager."

"Thanks." I palmed the keys and scrutinized Gary, wondering if he was a homosexual serial rapist or just a CIA agent that was going to need access to my apartment.

After double-checking to make sure my door really locked and that the keys worked, I walked down the hall and knocked on the Reynoza's door again. This time Julio answered.

"Whoa! Dude! How're you feeling?" Julio said when he opened the door. "Come on in."

"I'm doing good." I stepped inside his front door. Televisions were on in every room but he appeared to be alone.

"Can I get you something to drink? A beer?"

"I'm fine, I just had lunch."

"Did they catch the guys that got you?"

"Not yet. I'd like to ask you a few questions."

"Sure, sit down." Julio swept an empty potato chip bag and several Sports Illustrated magazines from the couch to clear me a spot.

"Thanks."

"What do you want to know?" He fumbled with a remote control, eventually muting the volume on the huge projection screen television in the living room that was tuned to live coverage of the

National Hot Rod Association's drag races in Las Vegas.

Elisha and I went to the drag races once. A friend of her brother's was crewing for one of the 'funny car' teams and had scrounged us a couple of free passes. The pit area was organized chaos as the team prepared the car. Her brother's friend explained that thousands of dollars went into the car before each run down the track, a ridiculously brief six-second event that covered the quarter-mile at speeds in excess of 250 miles per hour. Elisha didn't like the drag races. She thought that the bikini and wet t-shirt contests were degrading to women, the food terrible, men vulgar, and ultimately, the sound of uncorked racing engines revving to near destruction while spewing unburned fuel into the atmosphere was total sensory overload for her. Television just doesn't do NHRA drag racing justice, even on a big screen television with surround-sound.

"Are you sure I can't get you something?" Julio asked.

"I'm fine."

"I'm glad you're okay, you didn't look so good yesterday."

"I didn't feel good. Can you tell me what happened?"

"Sharon and I made a beer run and when we came back, we parked next to your car. There was a guy sitting in the front seat on the passenger's side, I thought he was a friend of yours. I said hello, but he didn't look up or anything."

"What did he look like?"

"I don't know, the window was rolled up and he was facing away, he didn't look at me. The lighting isn't that good down there."

"Then what happened?"

"We went over to the elevator and found you laying there. I'm telling you, I was sure you were dead, you were all gray and shit, you didn't move at all, there was a lot of blood. Sharon started screaming her head off, which didn't help me any."

"Was I unconscious?"

"I guess so, you weren't moving. I touched you and you felt cold. I thought about doing CPR."

"Why CPR?"

"I don't know, we all had to take a CPR course for the longshore union, and I didn't know what to do right away. Sharon was just screaming and screaming. I think the blood freaked her out."

"Did you dial 911?"

"Yeah, but I couldn't get reception on my phone near the elevator. There's a dead spot there, I had to walk over closer to the security gate."

"Then you dialed 911?"

"Yeah, and so then the 911 operator said the police were on the way and asked me to check to see if you had a pulse. When I went back over to you, my phone dropped the call and I had to dial 911 again and I got a different operator so I had to explain everything again. Sharon was totally freaking."

"I think I remember you talking to me."

"Yeah, I shook you and you sort of started coming to, but you were trying to hit me or something, and then you started throwing up all over the place. It was pretty fucking gross."

"What happened to the guy you saw in the car?"

"I don't know, I never saw him again."

My cell phone rang. Yeoman Jenkins told me I'd received a call from Captain Burns in Washington and that the information I'd requested from Coast Guard archives earlier in the day had just come in over the fax machine and it was marked 'Urgent.'

"Well, thanks for helping me," I said, standing to leave. The East Coast offices would be closing soon and I wanted to talk to Dan Burns before he went home. "You probably saved my life."

"I'm just glad you're all right." Julio Reynoza dug two twenty-dollar bills from his wallet and handed them to me.

"What's this for?" I asked.

"My friends ate your groceries," he said sheepishly. "Sorry, dude. They get hungry."

"No problem." Now I had a few bucks in my pocket until I could get a new cash card from the bank.

"I owe you another twenty, I'll catch you next time." Julio walked me to the door. "Oh yeah, there's something I didn't tell the cops last night," he added. "I just remembered."

"What's that?"

"Sharon was really freaked out, like I said, and it wasn't until later on last night that she told me about the other guy in the garage."

"What other guy?"

"There was another guy down in the garage last night."

"What did he look like?"

"She said he looked kind of like a Reggae singer."

"What do you mean by Reggae singer?"

"You know, the way he was dressed. And his hair."

"Did he have dreadlocks?"

"That's it," Julio said, his eyes brightening. "He had dreadlocks."

"What was he doing?"

"She said he was just sort of standing in the shadows watching us, but then he opened the security gate and walked out to the street. Real calm like."

16

As I drove back to the Coast Guard base, I mulled over the events of the last couple days, trying to make sense of it all. James Wierman had been beaten up and killed, but his wife was unhurt when they raided his house a couple hours later and took a framed photograph from the wall. I got hit from behind but Fat Louie had been tortured before they killed him. According to what Julio Reynoza just told me, it's possible that the two CIA agents I'd seen in the cargo hold of the *Balboa Victory* the of night James Wierman's murder were the same ones that attacked me in the parking garage of the Bonita Apartments. What were they after? It didn't make sense that they were looking for the letter Brooke Wierman gave me because a few hours after they had the letter in their possession, Fat Louie was unmercifully tortured to death. They had to be after more than the letter. Maybe they intended to kidnap me but Julio Reynoza and his screaming girlfriend scared them off. Did they finally get what they wanted from Fat Louie?   I'm guessing that they didn't.   Why would Fat Louie endure so much pain unless he couldn't give them what they were looking for?   Fat Louie didn't seem like the kind of guy that had a high tolerance for pain.   As for me, about the time they held bare electrical wires to my testicles, I'd have been sounding off like an auctioneer overdosing on speed.

What puzzled me was that even if they wanted the letter Brooke Wierman gave me, they could have simply taken it from my car when I was at the grocery store because it was over the sun visor the whole time.   They were obviously waiting in the parking garage for me to come home, and that meant they'd been monitoring my movements and had intentionally set me up.

After checking in with the sentry at the front gate of the Coast Guard base, I pulled around back and found a parking spot close to the building.   Why did they target me?   Did I know more about what they wanted and not even realize it?   Maybe I've come across something that means nothing to me, but is vital to them. What could it be?

Somehow they knew Brooke Wierman gave me an envelope, but probably didn't know what it contained, so it would make sense that they'd want to get their hands on it.   I tried to recall Brooke Wierman's exact words.   She hadn't been very specific during our phone conversation about what was in the envelope.   As a matter of fact, she hadn't even opened it, she just told me that her mother was looking in the safety deposit box for life insurance policies and found something addressed to the Coast Guard. The only way they could know that Brooke Wierman gave me an envelope was if they were listening to our phone conversation.

Yeoman Jenkins handed me a stack of papers as I passed by his desk. "James Wierman's service records are on top."

"Thanks." I closed my office door, threw the papers on my desk, and dialed the number for Captain Dan Burns in Washington. While waiting for the receptionist at the Marine Safety Office in Washington to connect me, I thumbed through Wierman's Merchant Marine service record.

James Wierman's first trip to sea as a ship's engineer was in June of 1963 as a third assistant on a freighter named the *Sea Ace*. In May of 1965 he had enough sea time and upgraded his license to second assistant engineer and in August of 1967 he obtained his first assistant engineer's license from the Coast Guard. We issued his chief engineer's license to him in San Diego on June 17th of 1969 and two weeks later he shipped out of San Francisco on the *S.S. SeaTrans Pride*, bound for Vietnam and Thailand. He sailed with SeaTrans until signing on the *SeaTrans Expeditor* and then he never served on another SeaTrans ship until he retired in 2007. The letter Wierman left in the safety deposit box said he'd been fired from the company. Apparently, he never did go back to work for SeaTrans. So why did he do it now? Why did he take the job on the *Balboa Victory,* an ex-SeaTrans ship, after all these years if he had such bitter feelings?

"You caught me just as I was leaving," Dan Burns said. "I have to be somewhere else right now so I don't have a lot of time."

"Let's make it quick then."

The sound of papers rustling came through the phone line. "Here it is," Dan Burns said. "The casualty of the *SeaTrans Expeditor* was investigated by Walt Jackson out of our Honolulu office. Apparently, after the crew was rescued in the South China Sea, they were flown to Honolulu before being repatriated. According to Walt Jackson's report, the *SeaTrans Expeditor* was lost due to sinking just like you said."

"Did he note any extenuating circumstances?"

"No. But he did suspend both the Captain's and the Chief Engineer's licenses for six months, which personally, I feel was a little extreme. In his report, he hammered them for trying to fix the ship at sea instead of turning back to a port in the Philippines to make repairs."

"Why do you feel the suspension was extreme?" I asked.

"Those ships came out of the mothball fleet. They'd been laid up the whole time after the Korean War until Vietnam and by then they were almost thirty years old. There were all kinds of problems with all the ships coming out of layup... boiler meltdowns, warped turbines, plugged fuel lines, trashed condensers, generator fires and sea valve failures. The problems experienced on the *SeaTrans Expeditor* were in line with problems on other ships that age and it certainly wasn't the first time a sea valve that had been underwater for thirty years finally caved in. I don't think you should punish a marine engineer when he's forced to work on a piece of junk and that piece of junk finally quits on him. I think James Wierman was doing the best he could under the circumstances."

"But he sank the ship on purpose and lied about it."

"Well, that definitely casts a different light on the casualty. If he were still alive, he'd be facing criminal charges."

"How about the statute of limitations?" I asked.

"There's not a statute of limitations on sabotage during wartime, it's similar to murder."

"Maybe somebody was blackmailing James Wierman and things got out of hand," I said.

"Blackmail for a forty year-old crime?" asked Dan Burns. "Wierman's career was over, he was retired, and even if somebody knew about what he did, it would be hard to prove it after all these years, especially since all the evidence is at the bottom of the ocean."

"But there would still be the criminal charges."

"Honestly, Jared, we probably wouldn't pursue it at this point, we have a lot fresher fish to fry."

"You've got a point, but I've still got a couple of murder cases on my hands," I said. "How about Walt Jackson? Is he around to talk to?"

"Sorry, he retired from the Coast Guard in 1982 and died in 1989," Dan Burns said. "But I did get a copy of the *SeaTrans Expeditor's* last crew list, and just by looking at crewmember birth dates, there's a few guys that might still be around."

Dan Burns gave me three names. I wrote down their ratings, social security numbers, and birth dates; all information routinely included on a crew list along with next of kin and home addresses.

"The chief mate should be about Wierman's age, so he might still be alive," Dan Burns said. "And the two midshipmen from the U.S. Merchant Marine Academy at Kings Point should be in their mid-fifties by now. I'll fax you the entire crew list tomorrow, but I checked the birth dates and unless you get real lucky, most of the others are probably dead."

Dan Burns said he had to go, he was already late, but asked me to let him know how it turned out.

Homeland Security has an extensive database and I soon discovered that one of the midshipmen from Kings Point, Harry McKeehan, had died two years ago. The other midshipman, Ralph Shafer, lived in Concord, New Hampshire where he worked for Schmitt Annuity and Life. There was no answer at his work number, it was after five on the East Coast, and when I tried his home phone, I got an answering machine but didn't bother to leave a message.

James Nolan, the chief mate on the *SeaTrans Expeditor* for her last voyage, now listed as retired from the International Maritime Union, was at home in Portland, Oregon and answered on the third ring. After I introduced myself, I asked him about the *SeaTrans Expeditor*.

"That was a lot of ships and a lot of years ago," James Nolan said, his voice crackling with old age. "I remember that ship because it was my very first chief mate's job. But I wasn't on her when she sank."

"You were on the crew list as chief mate," I said.

"I signed on in San Pedro with the rest of the crew, but when the ship sailed from Manila, I was in the hospital."

"Why?"

"It's a long story."

"Give me the short version."

James Nolan sighed. "We sailed from San Pedro and stopped in Honolulu if I remember right. We had a crew of drunks that trip and they were a nightmare."

"How so?"

"We were carrying pallets of beer in number two and number three cargo holds and the crew, both deck and engine, kept cutting the locks and stealing the beer. Finally, I used up all the locks I had and then paid somebody overtime to stay on deck at night to keep the rest of the crew from stealing beer, but that didn't work because the seamen I had on overtime to were in on it, too. There was a twenty-four hour a day poker game going on down in the crew's quarters and I had drunks staggering around up on deck. When we finally got to Manila, the schedule was really screwed up and there wasn't any room for us at the dock so we had to anchor out. A day or two after we anchored, a Navy lieutenant came out to the ship and told our captain that the ship's orders changed and we'd be offloading some cargo onto barges so we could shift other cargo around to different holds."

So far what James Nolan was telling me sounded consistent with Wierman's letter where he talked about the Navy placing a device in the hold of the ship.

"Since we were at anchor, we didn't have any longshoremen and our own crew had to unload the cargo with the ship's gear, but most of them were drunk and they were dropping pallets of beer into the harbor, on the barges, or each other. It was a total fiasco. We got rid of the beer and then things got really bad."

"Why's that?" I asked.

"Have you ever been around a bunch of drunks when they're drying out?"

"I can imagine," I said. "Did the captain do anything about that?"

"He was locked in his cabin most of the time. He didn't seem to care what happened, and if he did, he didn't do anything about it. He was probably drunk, too."

"How did you end up in the hospital?"

"After all the cargo work was done, it was still a couple of days until we were due to go to the dock and the Navy lieutenant offered to buy me dinner over at the officer's club. By then, I was up to my eyeballs with the bullshit on the ship so I went with him. We had a nice steak dinner, watched the USO show, and then he wanted to hit a couple of the strip joints in town before he took me back to the ship. We were coming out of one of the topless bars and we got jumped. I was stabbed three times in the stomach, they took my wallet with about two hundred bucks, and then they got away on a motorbike. I passed out on the street and almost bled to death."

"What happened to the lieutenant?"

"He took off after the motorbike and that's the last time I saw him. He never even came to see me in the hospital. After a few days in the Navy hospital in Manila, they flew me to Honolulu for a week or so before I went home. That's when I heard about the ship sinking."

"Did anything unusual happen while you were at anchor in Manila?"

"The whole damn thing was unusual if you ask me," Nolan said.

"Why's that?"

"Typical government fuck-ups," he said. "Nobody knew what was going on, and then the crew was fighting and seeing spiders and snakes as they dried out, that type of shit. It was definitely not a good voyage."

"You said a Navy lieutenant came out to the ship while you were at anchor and had you move cargo around," I said. "Did anything unusual happen during the cargo transfer, other than drunks dropping beer in the harbor?"

"Now that you mention it, there was something that bothered me at the time, but the whole damn thing was so screwed up that I didn't give it much thought until later."

"What's that?" I asked.

"Well, when you're down in those cargo holds, sound kind of travels around and sometimes you hear somebody that's fifty feet away and it sounds just like they're right next to you. That Navy lieutenant had a couple enlisted guys working with him and a few times I heard them call him Captain and he would make a face and shush them. There was that, and then he was always whispering to them like he didn't want anybody to hear. Usually, officers are yelling at the enlisted men and calling them all kinds of names. This guy didn't."

"When you heard them call him Captain, did you hear what name they used?"

"If I did, I don't remember it now," Nolan said. "But why would a guy that's a captain in the Navy be posing as a lieutenant?"

17

It was almost five-thirty on the East Coast and I tried Ralph Shafer's home phone number in Concord, New Hampshire, but got his answering machine again. I didn't leave a message but scribbled a note to myself so I wouldn't forget to try him at work tomorrow morning.

I stared at my phone and tried to decide how to proceed from here. My options were running out fast. Lloyd Waller had warned me off the case so he wasn't going to be any help. The CIA was probably implicated in my mugging and the murders of James Wierman as well as Fat Louie. Even if they didn't do it, they had a pretty damn good idea who did, which is probably why they were hanging around the harbor, but there's no way they are going to cut me in on what they knew. The San Pedro Police Department might be of some help since they'd caught the homicides, but they were too busy trying to cover street crime to really do me any good. Besides, with the FBI and CIA involved, the SPPD was way out of their league.

Popping open a Red Bull and downing the last of the pills Rachel Terazzo gave me this morning, I tried to muster the courage to make the phone I knew I needed to make. If I was going to step in shit, I might as well jump in with both feet.

My eldest brother, Michael, dealt more with the lobbying and political connections of the law firm while my other older brother, Edward, was better at the actual legal aspects. It was Michael that could help me and I punched up the number before I had a chance to chicken out.

"Stanton, Brugman, and Stroup," said a sweet young voice on the other side of the continent.

I was surprised the receptionist was still working, even though most of my brother's really productive business took place after hours and late at night. His days from eight to five were usually filled with politically motivated golf, tennis, handball, or cocktails.

"I'll see if he's in," she said after I explained who I was. I knew that she really meant, "He's in, I'll see if he wants to talk to you."

"Little brother," Michael said after I was on hold for only a few moments. "I heard you were in town over the weekend but you didn't stop by."

"I was really busy. I didn't even get a chance to see Mom."

"I heard you met with the budget sub-committee," he said. "How did that go?"

Nothing gets by my brother. "So-so."

"You should have let me know. I could've made some calls for you," he said. "We still need an investigator here at the firm. With your background, you'd be perfect for the job and you'd be making at least double what the Coast Guard is paying you," he added, trying to sound sincere instead of condescending.

Money isn't everything. I knew about the job because he'd offered it to me before. After the Boca incident. It involved delivering briefcases full of money or documents to congressional aides without being seen. Sometimes I'd be tracking a politician or one of his staff members, trying to take lurid photographs of them with a Congressional page or in the middle of a homosexual encounter. My brother tried to make it sound like a James Bond type of job, but I knew better. Washington politics is a vicious cutthroat business and I wanted no part of it. Maybe that's why my father said he was proud of me for what I'd done with my life. I'd managed to steer clear of the sewer and hadn't been sucked under by power or greed. Lust had been my personal downfall.

"Maybe. I'll let you know, but that's not why I called," I said, trying to quickly moving away from the subject. "I've got an active case you might be able to help me with."

Just asking for Michael's help after all these years made me realize the problems I had with my brothers stemmed from my own foolish pride. I'd never asked them for a damn thing. I'd been the black sheep of the family growing up, but a lot of that was my own choice. I didn't fully understand it, a lot was probably typical sibling rivalry and rebellion in the early years, but part of me didn't want to be included and I was too stubborn and prideful to admit it. Hell, I thought to myself, maybe my shrink was earning his money after all.

"Let's hear it, I'll see what I can do."

I started by telling him it involved the CIA moving gold during the Vietnam War just to make sure he would listen to the rest of it. After I had his attention, I filled him in about James Wierman's murder, the burglary, the confession letter, Fat Louie, lunch with Lloyd Waller and then how I'd been knocked senseless in the parking garage.

"That's interesting," Michael said, asking for clarification on the spelling of names as well as the dates and times of everything I could remember. That was probably the lawyer in him.

There was an awkward silence and audible shuffling of papers before said, "Our firm represented Sheridan and SeaTrans on a couple of things years ago."

"You did?"

"I'm not sure how much I can help you, but I can tell you what is common knowledge," he said. "I can't reveal anything that's confidential between the firm and SeaTrans."

"I'll take the common knowledge."

"It was in the newspapers, about 1998 or 1999, I'm not sure of the exact dates, but SeaTrans was involved in alleged kickbacks and bribes with one of the major shipyards out on the West Coast."

"Now that you mention it, I vaguely remember hearing something about that. Was that SeaTrans?"

"That's who it was," Michael said. "Some whistleblower complained, the FBI got involved, and supposedly they got Sheridan on videotape. The U.S. Maritime Administration was financing over ninety percent of the construction costs for twelve SeaTrans containerships at an allegedly inflated price and Sheridan, along with several top shipyard executives, were skimming excess profits so they could take a piece of the pie for themselves. Nothing was ever proven, and after awhile, it all just went away."

"Why didn't the FBI pursue it?" I asked.

"This is between you and me," Michael said. "I'll deny ever saying it. But that same shipyard also had a multi-billion dollar contract to supply the U.S. Navy with nuclear submarines and aircraft carriers. If criminal charges had been filed, it would have been devastating to both the shipyard management and the Navy. And you know how the Navy operates, the last thing in the world they want is for somebody to go snooping around and scrutinizing their shipbuilding contracts. They always keep that strictly hush-hush."

"So what finally happened?"

"Well, I think the fix was in because it finally turned out that the videotapes had been doctored, and therefore, they were inadmissible as evidence. All the charges were dropped and the FBI agents involved were reprimanded and transferred."

"How convenient," I said. "It must have taken a lot of political horsepower to pull that off without an all-out Congressional investigation."

"That's why we get the big bucks," Michael said. "Not long after that, SeaTrans had a problem with the Securities and Exchange Commission as they were taking the company public."

"What kind of problem?"

"Questionable accounting practices," Michael said. "Privately held companies can get away with more than those that are publicly traded. I don't know the specifics, I wasn't involved with that one, but I did pick up a little industry chatter."

"What do you know about the CIA operating SeaTrans during the Vietnam War?"

"I hadn't heard about that," Michael said. "It was a little before my time, but I'll make a few calls and get back to you."

We said our goodbyes and I promised to call before my next trip back East so we could get together. After I hung up, I noticed my hands were sweating and my collar was moist. As I tugged at my tie, I wondered if it was the Red Bull and Rachel's pills making me sweat, or if it was because I had been talking to my brother.

My thoughts turned back to my conversation with James Nolan, the chief mate on the *SeaTrans Expeditor* that was stabbed outside a strip joint while the ship was at anchor in the Philippines. Was it possible that the CIA was involved with his attack? They were certainly operating the *SeaTrans Expeditor* at the time. Did he see something during the cargo transfer that he shouldn't have and that's why he was brutally knifed and left on the street to die?

Suddenly something Dan Burns said this afternoon hit me like a ton of bricks. Not many crewmembers from the *SeaTrans Expeditor's* last voyage were still alive. Until just a couple of days ago the only ones thought to be alive were Wierman, Nolan, and Ralph Shafer. Wierman was just murdered, but Nolan was left for dead in the street over forty years ago. Was something going on that had the CIA covering their tracks after all these years?

I tried Ralph Shafer's home phone number one last time and got a busy signal. That was a good sign. Hopefully Ralph Shafer would stay alive until I could talk to him.

18

Thursday afternoon was muggy and still without even a hint of the usual sea breeze, a sure sign that the weather was about to change. The windows were rolled down on my government sedan as I crossed the Vincent Thomas Bridge for what I hoped was the last time today. The sun, enlarged by a Hevelian halo refracting light through atmospheric ice crystals, lingered low in the hazy but cloudless sky somewhere between the north end of Catalina Island and the historic lighthouse on Point Fermin. I glanced to the south and saw the *Balboa Victory* casting an inky shadow over the green waters of the main shipping channel. The late day sun made the old vessel look like a rust-ridden derelict waiting to sink at the dock.

Halfway across the bridge, I remembered my dry cleaning needed to be picked up by six o'clock. It was only a quarter to five and that meant I had time to stop by the Merchant Marine Veterans office to see if I could catch Frank Burch before he went home. Since he was the Chief Engineer on the *Dixie Victory* and had been the one that found James Wierman's body, he might also know why Wierman was so upset last week. At lunch, Lloyd Waller had told me, in so many words, to stay clear of the case and let the FBI handle it. But Rachel's pills and the Red Bull had worked up a full head of steam so I was presently fostering the attitude that Lloyd Waller could go screw himself.

There were four cars ahead of me at the bottom of the bridge exit ramp, but I could still see Reverend Johnny on his corner working the rush hour traffic. I drove straight through when the light changed and parked in front of the Merchant Marine Veterans office building.

There wasn't any coffee in the pot and only three sugared cake doughnuts left on the tray, but Frank Burch and two of his buddies were still in the office, leaning back in their chairs and telling each other sea stories.

Corrine, the secretary, was behind the counter and when she saw me walk through the door, her face twisted into an expression like she'd just caught me peeing on her rose bushes.

"I have a question about the main condenser on a Victory ship," I said. "Frank, maybe we can take a walk and you can show me."

As Frank and I crossed the parking lot on our way to the ship, I told him that the Marine Safety Office back in Washington was reviewing an old casualty report and needed a clarification about the cooling water setup on a Victory ship. Since they knew that the *Dixie Victory* was docked in

San Pedro and in excellent operating condition, they'd asked if I would take a quick look. Frank bought it.

There was a chain link gate at the bottom of the fenced in area around the gangway and Frank fumbled with a ring full of keys. He picked a key, tried it in the lock and when it didn't work, cursed under his breath and fumbled with his keys some more.

"Have they found out anything about who killed Jim?" he asked.

"I think they're still working on it," I said. "Do you have any ideas?"

"Not a clue."

"How well did you know him?"

Frank eyed me cautiously. "Those detectives treated me like I was a suspect," he said. "You didn't come down here to give me the third-degree did you?"

I held my hands up. "Not me. I've got nothing to do with it."

"Good." Frank found the right key and opened the lock to the gate.

Right away I could see that the *Dixie Victory* was in a lot better shape than her sister ship, everything was painted a shiny gray and the decks were kept free of dirt and trash. Frank fumbled with another lock on the main deck watertight door to the accommodation space. Inside, the passageways were adequately illuminated and immaculately painted. The entry to the engineroom was outside the crew's mess hall and I followed Frank as he descended into the bowels of the ship. The lower we went, the more pronounced was the distinctive smell of Bunker 'C', the high-sulfur fuel oil with the consistency of asphalt that is used on steam powered ships to fire the boilers.

"Here's the main condenser," Frank announced, pointing out a piece of equipment about the size and shape of a two-ton delivery van. "Cooling water comes in down below from the main sea chest and circulating pump, goes through the condenser, which has hundreds of tubes the water goes through, and then out the overboard discharge right there," he said, pointing at the two-foot diameter pipelines to trace the path of the cooling water for me.

I nodded.

"Steam from the turbines comes in from above, is cooled by the seawater inside the tubes where it turns back into water that we call 'condensate', and then the condensate is pumped into a tank so we can run it through the boilers again."

"How would a boiler get 'salted up'?"

"If one of the tubes had a hole in it, seawater would be mixed in with the condensate, and seawater is bad for boilers."

"What do you do about that?"

"The first thing we try is injecting sawdust into the cooling water."

"Sawdust?"

"Yep, if your leak is small enough, the sawdust will plug the hole and not let the seawater through."

"That works?"

"A lot better than you think it would. We always carry bags of sawdust when we go to sea."

"So condenser leaks are common."

"As common as hair on a dog."

"What would you do if that didn't work?"

"Well, you have to shut down the condenser and pull those inspection plates so you can find out which tube is leaking, and then you plug it so no more cooling water runs through it. When you get too many bad ones, you just have to go through and start replacing them, but that's usually a job that's done in the shipyard."

There were eight inspection plates about the size of manhole covers, each one held in place with a couple dozen or so heavy nuts and bolts. With one eye, I could see opening the main condenser was no easy task.

"So what happens if the inspection plates are off the condenser and the main cooling water shut-off valve starts leaking?"

"You're in deep shit, my boy."

"The Marine Safety Office is wondering how long it would take to fill the engine room with seawater if the inspection plates were off the condenser and the sea water shut-off valve failed."

Frank looked around the engine room. "Not long. I wouldn't want to find out though."

I made a show of putting notes in a small book and then put it in my jacket pocket.

"This is a nice looking engine room," I said.

Frank beamed. "Thanks."

"You guys must spend a lot of time down here to keep it this nice."

"Well that, and we only take the ship out to sea for tours six or eight times a year."

"That must be fun."

"It's a kick in the ass to run these old ships, they don't make them like this anymore, and besides, none of the kids that go to sea these days know how to run them. When us old guys die off, I don't know who they'll get to sail them."

"That's going to be a sad day."

"Got that right."

"By the way, I don't mean to change the subject, but I was on the *Balboa Victory* the other night and heard you talking about it being haunted."

It was the wrong thing to say because Frank looked embarrassed. "I should have kept my mouth shut," he said, his lips tense.

"I'm interested in why you said that."

Frank eyed me cautiously again. "Why?"

"A security guard up in Suisun Bay was found dead on the *Balboa Victory* a while back and I was just wondering why you said what you did."

Frank spent a moment considering his answer. "I was up there a year or so ago looking for spare parts for *Dixie*, that's what we call her, *Dixie*. That was before they decided to bring the *Balboa* down here," he said. "It was pitch-black on the ship and I was walking around with three flashlights, in case the batteries went dead on one of them, and I kept hearing footsteps, like heavy boots, and watertight doors closing, that type of thing, but I was the only one on the ship."

"Maybe it was the security guard."

"They didn't have a security guard then, the whole ship was locked up tighter than a drum and they gave me the only set of keys."

"Did you ever find out what it was?"

"No, but it gave me the heebie-jeebies. I just kept thinking about those guys getting killed in the cargo hold."

"I'll bet it shook you up to find James Wierman the other night."

"No shit."

"Did you know him for a long time?"

Frank gave me another cautious look. "Why?"

"Just curious I guess. The whole thing seems strange."

Frank paused. "I've known Jim off and on for thirty years, we'd run into each other around the union hall or around town sometimes. We weren't bass fishing buddies or anything, but he was a good guy and we got along."

"Do you know what he was working on over on the *Balboa*?"

"Mostly just getting ready for the shipyard, making a list of things he wanted done."

"Did he do any painting?"

"I don't think so."

"I noticed that the machine shop was freshly painted."

"They did that up in Suisun Bay."

"Who did?"

"A painting crew sent up there by SeaTrans."

"Why."

"Did you notice all those boxes down in the hold?"

"Yeah."

"They're full of spare parts and were supposed to be stacked in the machine shop before the ship was towed down from up north, so they wanted the deck painted first. That was going to be a storage room, but they didn't get the boxes aboard before the ship left and SeaTrans ended up trucking them down here instead."

"Why didn't the boxes get put on the ship?'

Frank shrugged. "Typical MARAD operation, I guess. The Maritime Administration could fuck up a dog's funeral, but I guess you being with the Coast Guard and all, you'd know that already."

I forced a cautious smile and carefully considered my next question. "I heard James Wierman was upset a week or so before he died. Do you have any idea if he was mad at anybody."

"I don't think he was mad, but he was kind of annoyed with one of the SeaTrans port engineers because they'd deleted a bunch of his shipyard items from the list. He told me they said they didn't have money to do the required work and that the volunteers would have to take care of it. He felt that some of the repair items should be taken care of by the shipyard because they were too complicated for the volunteers to handle."

"Who is the port engineer?"

"Some kid named George Rogers, a nice enough kid, but he don't know shit about these old steam ships."

"So Wierman was annoyed with George Rogers for canceling repair items he wanted done in the shipyard?"

"Jim came over here one afternoon to talk to me. He'd gotten the shipyard list back and wanted my opinion before he went up to the SeaTrans office to talk to them."

"So he was going to talk to George Rogers about the shipyard list?"

"Well, actually, it turned out that it wasn't George Rogers that crossed the items off the list," Frank Burch said. "It was Malcolm Cross."

19

Cobb Salad was the dinner special at the Harbor Light and I was going to order one if Stan ever got done arguing with the chowderhead whose credit card had just been declined by the Harbor Light's cashier.

My favorite stool was empty when I came in and now I was listening to the argument while I tried to decide if I was really being followed. The black Chevy Tahoe I suspected of tailing me had been parked alongside the road under the Vincent Thomas Bridge. I'd finished talking to Frank Burch on the *Dixie Victory* and was on my way to pick up my dry cleaning when I first spotted it. The traffic light on Harbor Boulevard had taken forever to change and I was mindlessly drumming my fingers on the steering wheel when I saw the black Tahoe just sitting alongside the road. When I took a left onto Harbor, it pulled into traffic about six or seven cars back and was still in my rearview mirror as I took a right onto 22nd Street to go up the hill. Three-quarters of a mile later it had still been behind me. A silver Honda's tinny horn resonated the driver's displeasure when I'd made a right turn on the red light at 22nd and Western Avenue, cutting cut him off so I could get some separation from the Tahoe. The Honda then followed me the twelve blocks up Western Avenue to the strip mall dry cleaners and the driver had rolled down his window to verbally abuse me after I parked my car.

"Sorry," I'd said to the teenage boy that had a girl in the car with him. "You had the right of way, I don't know what I was thinking."

The teen had continued to stream obscenities at me as I walked away, he wasn't the least bit nullified by my apology. Finally I'd heard the girl say, "Let's just go."

There was a black SUV at the far end of the parking lot when I exited the dry cleaners but I wasn't sure if it was the same one I thought had been following me initially. Just in case it was, as soon as I'd left the parking lot, I made a series of quick evasive turns in the residential neighborhood behind the mall before I pulled to the curb to find out if the Tahoe would drive by. If it really had been the CIA, and they wanted to track my movements, all they had to do was activate the GPS tracking device in my government car and then focus a satellite on me.

Because of the credit card fiasco, Stan had a scowl on his face when he finally brought my usual double shot of Jack Daniels and can of Seven-Up.

"No alcohol for me tonight."

"Why?"

"Head injury." I showed him my scalp and then filled him in on the details of the parking garage attack, hospital visit, and the pills I was taking.

"If you're not drinking, then what're you going to have?"

"The Cobb Salad and a glass of white wine."

"White wine has alcohol."

"Are you a chemist or a bartender?" I said deadpan before cracking a wry smile to show I was joking.

Stan wasn't amused by my joke and didn't say anything when he brought my wine. I assumed he was still pissed off about the credit card hassle.

"You're predictable," Rachel Terazzo said as she slipped onto the bar stool next to mine. "You shouldn't be drinking."

"It's only white wine."

Rachel rolled her eyes.

"You're as bad as my pharmacist."

Rachel stole a sip of my wine a made a face. "If you're going to drink wine, at least order something decent. This is awful."

"You hungry?" I asked. "I'm having a Cobb Salad."

"Nah," Rachel said. "I ate a while ago."

"What's up?" Because of Rachel's comment, I swirled the wine in my glass to see if it had legs. It didn't, and Rachel looked troubled.

"Tomorrow is my last day," she said.

"What?" Her statement hit me like a truck and I wasn't sure how I felt. Why was she leaving? Did it have anything to do with her suitcases being packed? There was nothing between us romantically, but still I felt close to her and now there was a gnawing emptiness in my stomach at the thought of her leaving.

Rachel was studying my reaction to her comment but looked away when I caught her.

"Administrative leave," she said. "I have to work with the prosecutors on the snuff film case and the department doesn't want me on the street until it's over."

"You're coming back after the trial aren't you?"

She shrugged and looked towards the front door.

I took a gulp of wine to drown the butterflies in my stomach but it didn't work.

"I don't know if you've heard yet, but we got pulled off the Wierman murder case this afternoon," she said.

"What?"

"Lieutenant Richards got a call from downtown and we're off the case."

"What does that mean?"

"That means we don't go near it. Somebody else is handling it."

"Who?"

Rachel shrugged again.

I drank more wine and then signaled for Stan to bring me another.

"Take it easy with that stuff," she said. "Mixing wine with those pills I gave you will knock you on your ass."

"Like I'm not on my ass already?" The slow burn started in my frontal lobe but rapidly became a raging inferno that consumed my whole body. Rachel had drawn me into this case and now that I was involved, she was backing out. I'd wanted no part of this stupid murder case in the first place. Then the injustice of being attacked from behind in the parking garage began fueling my anger. Nobody cared that I'd almost been killed. Two people were dead and I was almost the third and nobody cared. Not the FBI, not Rachel, not my brother. I felt my face flush red.

"Are you okay?" Rachel asked.

"Fine." My ears were so hot I thought they'd burst into flames.

Stan brought my new glass of wine and I took a sip. It's the concussion and the pills I told myself. Get a grip on yourself. Just get a fucking grip on yourself Stanton.

I took several deep breaths. "I had an interesting lunch," I said, trying to compose myself by getting my mind on something else. After all, it wasn't Rachel's fault she'd been pulled off the case or put on administrative leave. Both her and Lieutenant Richards had to take their orders. That's how it works.

"What do you mean?" she asked. "What happened?"

As I told Rachel about Lloyd Waller, the CIA operating SeaTrans during the Vietnam War, and the gold shipment that might have gone to the bottom of the South China Sea, I could feel myself cool down and become more rational. Rachel sat sideways on her barstool, eyes fixed on me, right elbow on the bar with her chin resting in the palm of her hand. By the time I finished telling about my afternoon, I was fairly calm and Rachel was deep in thought.

"Now I think I'm being followed," I said.

"How do you know?"

I explained about the black Chevy Tahoe and how I'd ducked into a residential neighborhood just in case they were still following me.

"Are you sure it was a Tahoe?"

"Pretty sure. Why?"

"That wouldn't work anyway," she said, a distant thoughtful glaze to her eyes as she swirled the wine in my glass. "The timings all wrong."

"What do you mean?"

"We recovered a black Cadillac Escalade that was involved in Fat Louie's murder," Rachel said. "The bartender next door to the pawnshop gave us a decent description to go with a partial license plate number and we were able to match them up. The Westminster police found the vehicle over in Little Saigon in a parking lot."

"Who owns it?"

"That's not going to help us much, the owner reported it stolen the night of the murder."

"How convenient."

"We checked the guy out, he runs a plumbing supply store in Anaheim and was at dinner with his wife when his Escalade was stolen from the Sizzler's parking lot."

"Maybe he had a early dinner and then went over to execute Fat Louie for dessert."

"I don't think so," Rachel said. "The timing is wrong, and besides, it was his seventeenth wedding anniversary."

"He drives a Cadillac Escalade and takes his wife to a Sizzler for dinner on their anniversary?"

"Makes you want to run right out and get married doesn't it?"

"The guy's an idiot."

"Maybe, but either he's smarter than he acts or his Cadillac really was stolen. The driver's window had been slim-jimmed, alarm disabled, and ignition punched. We're running it for prints now."

"Anaheim is forty minutes away from San Pedro. You're telling me that somebody jacked a car in Anaheim, drove all the way to San Pedro, tortured Fat Louie to death, and then drove to Little Saigon, which is another forty minutes? Couldn't they have stolen a car a little closer to the crime scene?"

"The Sizzler was in Westminster and they found the Cadillac less than a mile from where it was stolen. Our 'perps' are probably from that area."

"This gets stranger by the minute."

Stan brought my Cobb Salad and when I saw the way Rachel looked at it, I asked him to bring another plate and a fork.

"On the subject to fingerprints," Rachel said. "We matched two sets of prints in Wierman's car to two Cabrillo Vo-Tech kids, and they just happened to be in the system."

"For what?"

"Being stupid," she said. "They got busted smoking dope, drinking beer, and littering down by Point Fermin lighthouse last year. Since it was their first arrest, they ended up getting probation, community service, and an ass-chewing from the judge."

"Do you think they were involved in the murder and stealing Wierman's car?"

"They said Wierman gave them the keys and sent them to the hardware store," she said. "We checked with that marine hardware store over in Wilmington and the guy remembers them coming in. He said they were goofing off and taking forever to get what they came for so he had his eye on them."

"How about that Canetti kid that was selling junk to Fat Louie? Did he ever show up?"

"He's still on his uncle's fishing boat as far as we know. The day shift checked it out earlier."

"I've got a question for you." I slid some of my salad onto the extra plate for Rachel. "How did they know I was in possession of a letter James Wierman wrote and why did they wait for me in the parking garage at my apartment building instead of taking it from my car at the grocery store or while we were talking to Fat Louie?"

"I've thought about that." Rachel forked through the salad looking for bacon and bleu cheese. "I figure they have the phones bugged."

"Mine or Wierman's?"

"Probably Wierman's," she said. "Maybe yours, too."

"So you're thinking it's the CIA?" I looked for confirmation in her face but didn't get it. "Why didn't they just walk up and ask to look at the letter, I'd have shown it to them. Hell, I would have made them a photocopy, I was going to give you one."

"They obviously don't want you to know what's going down." She pointed her fork at me while she chewed. "Which tells me that they have something to hide."

The wine had started to slow my thinking. "Are you talking about a cover-up?"

Rachel shrugged her shoulders, sipped my wine, and then made a face to let me know the new glass wasn't any better. "I have a plan. If you up for it."

"I'm pissed off. I'm up for it."

"What if Brooke Wierman were to call you and say she found a notebook her father had been keeping concerning the *Balboa Victory*?" Rachel said. "If they still have the phones bugged, they would know you had something else of Wierman's, and they would want to get their hands on it to find out what he'd been writing down."

"That sounds like a plan where I get the crap beat out me again, and I gotta' tell you, your pills work good, but not that good."

"We'll be waiting for them this time."

"We? Who do you mean by 'we'? I thought you were off the case."

"We're off the murder case, but the department is still handling the burglary."

"Is that your case?"

"Not really."

"Correct me if I'm wrong, but they're putting you on administrative leave. Won't you get in trouble?"

"What are they going to do to me?"

"What if the whole house is bugged? Won't they hear you explaining your little plan to Brooke Wierman?"

"I've thought about that and I've got it covered." Rachel held up a cherry tomato she'd stabbed with her fork. "Are you in?"

"Why not?"

"Good." She slipped off her barstool. "I have to go to work now, but I'll take care of it. Brooke Wierman will be calling your office at ten o'clock tomorrow morning. Be there."

"Tomorrow?   I thought you were on administrative leave."

"I am, but that means I'll have some free time."

"I've got another question."

"What's that?"

"Why would Lieutenant Richards get a call from uptown pulling him off the Wierman murder but not the Wierman burglary?"

"I don't know?"

"Maybe the two aren't connected," I said. "Or maybe they want us to think they aren't connected."

"Who knows," she said. "But I've got to get to work, we'll talk about it later."

Rachel leaned in a pressed something into my hand.

"What's this?"

"A key to my place, you'll be safer there until this is over with."

"I don't know where you live, I was kind of out of it when you took me there."

She wrote her address on a bar napkin, folded it, and then stuffed it in my shirt pocket. "You have my cell number," she said, touching my arm. "And don't drink too much."

I watched as she walked away and just before she went out the door she turned back to face me.

"Jared."

"Yeah?"

"Make sure you put the toilet seat down this time."

"Gotcha."

20

Sometimes a dream is just a dream.

Dan Burns and I were rowing on the Potomac River in the eight-man boat with some of his friends when the passing Presidential yacht hailed us. The yacht captain said the President was out of the country and they were going to a beach party. When we asked if we could come, he tossed us a towline. There were hundreds of people milling on the beach and my father dropped by to scold me about my grades. Rachel Terazzo and two girlfriends were dressed in black leather and had some guy in his underwear on a leash. Elisha brought me a plate of food and as we ate, we began to argue. She wanted to know if Rachel was my new girlfriend and the more I tried to explain, the madder she became until she stormed off to go swimming. The surf was heavy on the beach, which was strange because the river was the Potomac, but soon Elisha was drowning and calling to me for help.

I awoke with a start and found that the sound of the crashing surf in my dream was actually the snow on Rachel's television set. I'd fallen asleep on her couch watching an extra innings Angels-Red Sox game being played in Anaheim and the station had gone off the air.

After being forced to punch buttons on the front of the television to turn it off because I couldn't find the remote control, I flopped on the couch and tried to fall asleep again but there was an intense throbbing inside my head that was surely blood leaking out of my brain. A few minutes of the pain was all I could stand before I staggered into the bathroom to gulp another round of Rachel's pills. Back on the couch, I wondered what Elisha would really think of Rachel. I felt like I was cheating on her all over again.

It was just past four in the morning and there was no way I was going to be able to fall asleep again so I went into the kitchen to start a pot of coffee. Rachel had done some grocery shopping and left me a note saying I could help myself. Behind the fresh half-gallon of milk in her refrigerator was an eight-pack of Red Bull and I took one. Was that sour milk still in my own refrigerator or had I thrown it out? Julio Reynoza's friends had eaten all my groceries so I was sure the status my of my refrigerator was unchanged.

Bringing the Red Bull into the bathroom with me, I took a long steamy shower and by the time I dried off with one of Rachel's beach towels, the pills had kicked in. Rachel had laundered the sweat pants I'd worn when I was discharged from the hospital and left them folded at the foot of her bed. Barefoot and naked from the waist up, I went through an abbreviated workout in her spare room, letting the throbbing in my head dictate the pace.

The morning news started at five and I choked down two pieces of buttered whole-wheat toast along with three cups of black coffee while I watched television and put on a clean uniform. It turned out to be the same news, just a different day. By five-thirty it was starting to get light outside and I decided to borrow some workout gear down at the fireboat station so I could go rowing.

I left Rachel's key and a short handwritten note on the table, checked to make sure the toilet seat was down, and then stepped out of her apartment into the dawn to face a brand new paranoia filled day.

My eyes were glued to the rearview mirror as I drove down Pacific Coast Highway from Redondo Beach toward San Pedro Harbor and in less than thirty minutes I was outside the security gate at the firehouse. I reached for my wallet and swipe card, remembered they'd been stolen, and then punched in my personal five digit security code on the keypad. The parking lot was full of cars but nobody was around and the fireboats were gone. At first I thought they might have responded to a ship fire or oil spill but then I remembered it was Friday morning, the day that *Gypsy Of The Sea,* a new Denmark Line mega-cruise ship making her maiden voyage, was due to arrive in San Pedro

Harbor. The fireboats would be escorting the cruise liner to her berth, firing their water cannons in the air, the misty arcs of water celebrating the new ship's arrival to our fair harbor. I'd personally signed the order to double the number of Coast Guard escort vessels and Sea Marshals for the vessel's arrival as an increased security precaution for the high profile event that would be making the evening news on local television.

The firemen had all padlocked their lockers when they left on the fireboats so I was having trouble finding something to wear. Fortunately, I had the foresight to bring the sweatpants from Rachel's and then was able to find a SPFD t-shirt and windbreaker lying around the upstairs bunkroom. In the boathouse, I yanked the felt liners from a pair of rubber fire boots that had been left behind. I had just slipped the cover from my boat, the felt liners warm but clumsy on my feet, and was thinking to myself that maybe I should go barefoot, when I heard someone call my name.

I'd thought I was alone in the boathouse and since I was already a little paranoid, the voice startled me. I whipped my head around and faced a man, not more than fifteen feet from me, wearing a navy blue raincoat over a dark gray suit.

"I knew your father," he said, slowly coming closer, moving with a slight limp, his creased lips quivering slightly when he spoke. His eyes were as blue as a South Pacific lagoon; his gaze penetrated me with hawk-like intensity.

"You startled me."

"I'm sorry." He smiled politely.

The stranger looked to be in his sixties or well-preserved seventies, immaculately groomed, less than six feet, and moved with arthritic knees. He didn't offer to shake hands but rather had those blue eyes locked on me like a cat on a mouse. It crossed my mind that he might be an assassin, old men and beautiful women make great assassins because nobody expects them. I moved toward the edge of the dock where I could go into the water if he pulled a weapon.

"I'm sorry we have to meet like this," he said, glancing at the felt boot liners on my feet. "But your brother has been making some interesting inquiries on your behalf."

"Jared Stanton," I said, offering to shake hands, relaxing a little. "I was about to do a little rowing."

He didn't introduce himself or return my handshake offer, but instead, glanced behind me, surveying the harbor in the background.

"Maybe we can talk inside," he said.

"Sure." I kept an eye over my shoulder while I shuffled from the covered boathouse into the fire station crew lounge, the felt liners on my feet threatening to trip me.

"I'd offer you something to drink but..."

He waved me off with a slight hand gesture. "I only have a few minutes."

The stranger motioned for me to be seated on one of the couches, then he moved against the wall where he could face the door while he remained standing.

Paranoia welled up inside me. If he pulled a weapon I would be a dead duck sitting on the couch. The crime scene photos of me in sweat pants, SPFD windbreaker, felt liners on my feet, and a bullet hole in my forehead flashed through my mind.

"So what..." I started.

"I knew your father," he said. "And your brother has been asking questions that have a number of people disturbed."

"The gold?"

He nodded, his eyes never leaving mine. "And other things."

If he were going to kill me, he'd have already done it. I didn't even see him come in the boathouse; he could have taken me at anytime.

"You serve your country, Jared," he said. "You're in the Coast Guard and you worked for the FBI. Honorable service."

The stranger looked at the door again and then moved over to sit in a brown armchair opposite me, a hint of pain registering in his eyes, and some type of palsy causing random quivers around his mouth and eyes.

"This is a great country, Jared. The best. Unfortunately, there are those that want to take it from us, and as servants of the people, it is our job to prevent that from happening," he said. "Sometimes people don't understand what the government has to do to protect our way of life. Do you understand that, Jared?"

"Of course."

"The average person in this country lives from paycheck to paycheck. If they missed a payday or two, the electricity went off for a week, or there happened to be an interruption in the food supply, it would be bedlam in streets. Can you just imagine the grocery stores running out of food?"

I nodded.

"Most people don't think beyond what they're going to do this weekend, unless it's to plan a summer vacation. They don't plan financially or strategically in their lives. Consumer debt is a prime example of this." He paused for a moment to sigh and collect his thoughts. "But the government, Jared...the government doesn't have that luxury. We must not only handle the day to day needs of our citizens, but must also plan five, ten, twenty, even fifty years into the future so we can maintain the level of comfort everyone enjoys in this country. That's not an easy thing to do."

"Where are going with all this?"

"The war in Vietnam, Jared. Did we lose it?"

"Pretty much got our butts kicked."

"Did we?" he asked. "What is Vietnam like today and how significant is communism in our current global economic picture?   The Soviet Union is gone, the Chinese are embracing capitalism, just look at what is happening in Hong Kong since Great Britain turned it over to them, and if not for the ranting of feeble little North Korea, communism would be extinct. How has the world changed in just thirty years?"

"What does this have to do with gold?"

"I'll get to that in a minute," he said. "The average American eats fast food and judges wins and losses by sporting events that last mere hours.   We're mired in a struggle in the Middle East.   But how do you tell the average American that the final whistle doesn't blow in sixty minutes, but instead, it may blow in thirty, forty, or fifty years?   Maybe not even in their lifetime, or their children's lifetimes, for that matter.   They can't even begin to comprehend something like that, Jared."

My feet were beginning to sweat so I kicked the felt liners off my feet.   The stranger eyed me cautiously.

"We try to maintain a moral standard in this country, Jared, and the American public expects us to live up the standards we set.   But in real life, where there are subverted crusades that want to destroy our very way of life, we don't have the luxury of strictly adhering to those lofty standards."

"Like with Manuel Noriega in Panama or the drugs for arms in Nicaragua?"

"Just two examples, of course. But you get the point.   When we battle immoral forces, sometimes we must engage those forces on their own level, a level most Americans would find unacceptable and quite reprehensible."   The stranger paused to catch his breath.   "There are certain things the general public doesn't really need to know, nor is it practical to tell them every detail.   Certain events would surely cause catastrophic destabilization.   For instance, does the general public really need to know the truth behind John F. Kennedy's assassination, or is it enough for them to think Lee Harvey Oswald did it?   Did they need to know the truth then, and is it really relevant today? Would they understand that our role in the Middle East might extend more than fifty years? What would they say? If they knew the truth it would create chaos and a complete loss of confidence in the government. How can these minds that barely survive from week to week even begin to understand national strategic long-range goals or the protracted effort and commitment necessary to accomplish them? We only want what's best for the country and to maintain the American way of life."

"You're saying that the end justifies the means?"

"A little simplistic, but yes, Jared, that's exactly what I'm saying. It's an unfortunate reality, but many sacrifices in the short-term pay huge dividends in the long-term. Your father understood the principle all too well."

"How well did you know my father?"

"That's not the point."

"What is the point?"

"The point is that even in the best laid plans, certain details go awry, or certain personnel problems crop up. That doesn't mean we failed or that our plans were ill conceived. Just because a tire goes flat on a car, you don't scrap the entire vehicle and forget about your ultimate destination."

"Is that what's going on here?"

"Exactly," he said. "You've heard the saying, 'Let sleeping dogs lie'?"

"And that's what you want me to do?"

"Yes."

"I'd like to know what's really going on."

"It's a long story."

"I have time."

The stranger studied me for a few moments.

"You want to know about the gold?" he asked.

"To start with."

"How's that going to help you?"

"You want me to stop looking into this. I want to know what's going on if I'm going to drop it. I almost got killed and I want to know why."

The stranger sighed, his eyes focused on me. He looked tired.

"After World War Two," he began. "The United States was the world's economic and manufacturing powerhouse. When peace was finally established, vast regions of Europe and Japan were in ruins and their national economies destroyed as a result of the fighting, so we undertook rebuilding the economies and infrastructure of not only our allies, but our enemies as well. At that time, to maintain control of global economic growth and inflation, world currencies were tied to our dollar, and our dollar was backed by gold at a predetermined value. By the late sixties, the European and Japanese economies had recovered to the extent that the United States was experiencing trade deficits for the first time in history and the system that worked so well during the reconstruction period after World War Two, needed to be changed."

"To a flat currency." This was right in line with what Lloyd Waller told me.

"You know your history, Jared." The stranger paused to catch his breath. "The War in Vietnam and the social reform programs of that era were extremely costly, but increased taxation would only lead to even greater trade deficits and rampant inflation. The decision was made to convert to a flat currency instead of one based on the gold standard, and as a result, we had a huge accumulated asset, gold, that was essentially worthless to us. Those in charge of the war in Vietnam discovered that they could keep ten very well equipped local soldiers in the field for what it cost to keep one American serviceman. The war was not popular here in the States, as you well know, and so a strategic plan was drawn up whereby gold would fund the war effort using mercenary forces instead of American youth. Gold that had once been valued at the set price of thirty-five dollars an ounce, could be traded openly in Europe, primarily France, for hundreds of dollars an ounce. It was a win-win situation. The war could be fought without detrimental effects to our economy or loss of American lives."

"So what happened?"

"Like I said, the plan was sound, but the execution of it was somewhat flawed and that led to near catastrophic circumstances and ultimately the downfall of the presidency."

"Nixon?"

The stranger nodded.

"Correct me if I'm wrong, but wasn't it Watergate that led to Nixon's resignation?"

"Again, Jared," he said, looking tired. "Does the American public, or the rest of the world for that matter, really need to know the truth? What would happen if they knew there was no gold in Fort Knox? Would their lives be better today by simply knowing the truth? Do you really think President Nixon resigned because of blank spots on a tape and a few allegedly overzealous Republican Party members? He could have used any second-rate country lawyer to be exonerated from those flimsy allegations."

"We deserve the truth from our government."

"And you get it. Most of the time."

"So what about the gold?"

"Unfortunately, some of those working for the government were not the most reliable. Deficiencies developed in the logistics and some of the gold ended up in the wrong hands. Greed is always a powerful and unpredictable element that can tempt even the most loyal public servants."

"Somebody stole a million and half ounces of gold?"

"No, Jared. Two shipments consisting of a million and a half ounces each were sent to Vietnam as scheduled." He sighed. "The shipment aboard the *SeaTrans Expeditor* when it went to the bottom of the South China Sea was intended to turn the tide for us in Vietnam once and for all. It was a shipment of ten million ounces."

21

By the time I got to work I had three phone messages from my brother and an invitation from Denmark Line's Operations Superintendent to attend brunch aboard the *Gypsy Of The Sea.*

Michael answered his cell phone right away. "Run, little brother," he said. "Run, don't walk, away from whatever you're looking into."

"Did you find out what's going on?"

"No," he said. "I made a few calls using the information you gave me and about two hours later I was contacted by a source that sits on the National Security Council. He wanted to know why I was looking into the *SeaTrans Expeditor* incident and I told him what you told me."

"So what'd he say?"

"He told me to tell you, in the strongest terms possible, to quit your investigation and forget anything you've found out so far."

"That's what he said? Quit the investigation?"

"In the strongest terms possible, Jared."

"I had a surprise visit this morning from somebody that told me the same thing."

"Who was it?"

"I don't know," I said. "He never gave me his name, but he said he knew Dad."

"You better listen to him," Michael said. "I've got a meeting now, but promise me you'll drop this. Okay?"

"Sure."

Logic told me to leave it alone, and for about twenty minutes, while I sifted through the morning's duty rosters and harbor security alerts, I did. Whatever was going on got three people killed so far, at least those were the ones I knew about. There might be more victims out there somewhere that hadn't been linked to this thing yet and I didn't want to be added to the list of mysterious deaths. The events of the last couple days began to nettle me, like a mosquito bite you know you shouldn't scratch, but you just can't help yourself. The more you try to ignore it, the more it bothers you. Maybe there was a way I could find out what got James Wierman and Fat Louie killed without drawing attention to myself.

I began by making a list of all the people I knew that were associated with either the *SeaTrans Expeditor* or the *Balboa Victory* so I could cross-reference them. When I got to Ralph Shafer, the midshipman that had been aboard the *SeaTrans Expeditor* when she sank, I remembered I needed to call him again.

"Schmitt Annuity and Life," said a female voice.

"I'd like to speak with Ralph Shafer."

"May I say who's calling?"

"Commander Stanton of the U.S. Coast Guard."

"Just a moment please."

A click put me on hold and Carly Simon began crooning *You're So Vain* in my ear. It wasn't more than thirty seconds before Ralph Shafer came on the line.

"The Coast Guard is developing some ship casualty statistics," I told him after he introduced himself. "I was wondering if you could shed some light on the loss of the *SeaTrans Expeditor* in 1971."

"Wow," he said. "There's a name I haven't heard in years."

That was a good response and it told me that nobody had been in touch with him recently about the ship.

"The *SeaTrans Expeditor* was my first and last trip to sea," he said. "The experience was enough to convince me I wasn't cut out for a life in the Merchant Marine."

"Do you remember any details of the actual sinking?"

"Not really. Like I said, it was my first trip to sea and I'd only been aboard the ship a few weeks so I wasn't that familiar with the engineroom. They just had me running back and forth with tools. I remember we took our usual coffee break at ten in the morning and were sitting in the mess hall when the lights flickered several times and then went out. The silence was eerie."

"How long did it take for the ship to sink?"

"I'm not sure. We were in the lifeboat and it was my job to help with the motor and we had trouble getting it started so I was busy with that and then somebody threw up on me. Once that first person got sick, it was a chain reaction. The sea looked really calm from the ship but once we got in the lifeboat, it was a lot rougher than it looked."

"So you don't know how long it took the ship to sink?"

"No," he said. "By the time I got around to looking up, it was gone. I don't mind telling you, it's really intense having a ship sink out from under you. It changed my life."

Ralph Shafer didn't have much to else to add concerning the sinking of the *SeaTrans Expeditior*, other than he did say the FBI had grilled both him and the other midshipman extensively after they got rescued and were repatriated back to the States. I thanked him for his time and went back to compiling my list of names.

It was ten o'clock sharp when Yeoman Jenkins informed me that I had a phone call from Brooke Wierman.

"Mom and I were going through some of dad's clothes before taking them to Goodwill and I came across a notebook he was keeping about the restoration of the *Balboa Victory*." Brooke Wierman sounded like she was reading lines from a script. "I wasn't sure what to do with it and thought maybe it would help with your investigation."

"Hold onto it," I said. "I'll be there in twenty minutes."

I called Rachel's cell phone on my way out the door to tell her where I was headed and by the time I pulled into the Wierman's cul-de-sac in San Pedro, Rachel's car was already parked in front of the house.

"I'm not so sure about this," I said and then gave her a thirty-second rundown on my meeting with the stranger at the fire station and the conversation with my brother.

Rachel shrugged. "Let's just see where this goes."

We didn't go inside the Wierman's house; we just stood on the front porch talking to Brooke.

"How's your mother doing?" Rachel asked, keeping an eye on the street behind us.

"Not bad," said Brooke, holding a black leather notebook in her hand. "I don't think it's really hit her yet. The funeral isn't until Sunday."

Rachel and I stood close together with our backs to the street to block the view when Brooke gave us the notebook. We thanked her for her help and headed back to our cars.

"They won't know which one of us has it," Rachel said, keeping the notebook inside her windbreaker.

"I've got a bad feeling about this," I said.

Rachel pressed her apartment key into my hand again as we approached her car. "You really should be staying at my place until this is over."

"What's the plan?" I asked. "How are you going to keep me from getting the shit kicked out of me again, or yourself for that matter?"

"Keep your eyes open and don't get caught alone."

"That's it?" I asked. "That's your plan? Keep my eyes open? I thought you were going to have me under surveillance or something."

"I'm on administrative leave," she said. "I can't get extra help, but we can watch each other's back."

"Rachel, it's not much of a plan, I don't want to end up like Fat Louie." I hadn't seen the crime scene photos but my imagination ran wild at the thought of his pants down around his ankles and his testicles fried with electricity.

"But we're ready for them this time."

"Yeah, well I figure they know we're going to be ready for them and they'll be ready for us, too."

"That's combat, Jared," Rachel said. "Lock and load, then go looking for the shit. When the firefight starts, you'll know what to do."

"You're damaged."

"I know."

***

Since I was already on that side of town, I made an appearance at the *Gypsy Of The Sea* where I was given an abbreviated tour of the navigation bridge before being escorted to the lavish brunch where I found a large percentage of my on-duty Coast Guard personnel making the most of the rare opportunity. I loaded shrimp onto my plate at the base of a massive ice sculpture that I think was supposed to be a swan but looked more like a seagull swooping down to pluck shrimp from the platter.

"Don't forget the bachelor party tonight," said Chief Petty Officer Swain, one of the senior Sea Marshal patrol boat operators. "Ensign Dunn won't forget tonight any time soon," he said lewdly, standing beside me and loading shrimp onto his plate to the brim.

"I forgot all about it."

"You're kidding," CPO Swain said, munching a shrimp from his plate.

"I was out of town last week. Where is it and what time?"

"It starts right after work over at Henry's Fish House in Long Beach, then it's over to Fantasy World for the strippers, and it'll go until we get Dunn drunk enough to put him on a plane to Mexico."

"You guys have no mercy." Ensign Dunn was a nice enough kid. He was our information systems officer that coordinated Homeland Security multi-agency intelligence relevant to vessels arriving in our district, but when it came to real life, he was without a clue. I wondered if I was as naïve when I was his age. Probably so.

"Hell, Commander, a guy only gets married a few times in his life. You have to make the most of them," Swain said with a laugh.

Meetings, pre-meeting meetings, operation schedules, and a conference call with Admiral Ballard and the Officer-in-Charge of Port Security for San Francisco concerning merchant vessel boarding protocol, filled my afternoon schedule. By five o'clock my head was killing me so I took another round of pills, changed out of my Coast Guard uniform into a set up blue jeans and a yellow pullover golf shirt that was in my locker and headed to the party in Long Beach.

Henry's Fish House was full of Coast Guard personnel when I got there, and judging by the behavior of a few, I guessed the party had started well before the workday ended. Poor Ensign Dunn already had one foot on a banana peel and the other foot on a flight to Mexico. It was going to be a long night for him.

By seven-thirty we'd pretty much worn out our welcome at Henry's so the gang piled into the two limousines that had been hired for the weekend and we set out for the strip club.

The only thing that kept Ensign Dunn from lapsing into a coma was the string of lap dances he was being treated to. Dunn's alcohol consumption was being closely monitored so he would last until midnight and the grand finale.

I'd just switched from Seven-Up to Red Bull when I felt my cell phone vibrating.

"Commander Stanton?" said the voice I could barely hear over the din in the club. "This is Chief Taylor down here on harbor patrol."

"Yes, Chief, what can I do for you?" I said, putting a finger in my other ear so I could block out the music and yelling.

"You left an order for us to call you know if we saw anything suspicious happening on the *Balboa Victory.*"

"Yes," I shouted into the cell phone.

"Well, Commander," said Chief Taylor. "You better come down and have a look."

22

Rachel met me at Berth 232 on Terminal Island, directly across the main ship channel from San Pedro, and together we boarded the white forty-six foot aluminum Coast Guard patrol cutter commanded by Chief Petty Officer Taylor, a weathered skipper known to run his boat by the book.

"What's happening, Chief," I asked.

"There's a Jacobs ladder hanging from the stern of the *Balboa Victory*," he said, handing me a pair of binoculars. "It wasn't there when we made our five o'clock tour but we passed by again a half-hour ago and the ladder was hanging over the side."

"Did you see anybody on the ladder or suspicious watercraft loitering in the area?" I asked.

"No, just the ladder," he said. "And like I told you, it wasn't there earlier this evening."

We cruised slowly along the eastside docks and I scoped out the *Balboa Victory* across the ship channel through the binoculars.

"Looks quiet over there," I said. "But the bottom of that ladder is almost in the water and that means it's rigged for a small boat, it's too close to the water for a harbor tug or pilot boat to use."

"What do you want to do, Commander?" asked Chief Taylor.

"Where's the other patrol boat?"

"Chief Burns has it outside the breakwater waiting to put a Sea Marshal team aboard an inbound ship that's due to arrive about 2100 hours."

"Which ship?"

Chief Taylor checked the Homeland Security computer printout. "The *M.V. Southwind*, it's a Panamanian flagged freighter headed to Berth 178 with a load of rolled steel."

"Let's change Chief Burns' orders. We'll have him come up the channel to back us up, but don't say anything specific over the radio, just have him come up here. Somebody may be listening in on our frequencies."

"What are you thinking of doing, Commander?"

"I'm thinking Detective Terazzo and I should climb that ladder and find out what's going on," I said. "But until the other boat gets here, we'll just sit under the Vincent Thomas Bridge and watch."

All was quiet on the *Balboa Victory* while we waited for backup and at ten minutes past nine in the evening, Chief Burns, a grizzled 28-year veteran of the Coast Guard, pulled his patrol boat alongside ours and tossed us a mooring line.

"Evening, Commander," Chief Burns said. "I thought you'd be at the party."

"I was," I said.

"How's young Ensign Dunn holding up?" he asked, flashing a broad smile.

I laughed and shook my head.

"Poor kid, he'll be learning a few things the hard way. I hope he can speak Spanish so he can find his way home," Chief Burns said. "So what's going on here?"

"We're going to climb that ladder hanging off the *Balboa Victory*," I said. "I want you and your crew to provide back-up if things get western on us. Keep a sharp lookout for small boats in the area, somebody might be hiding between the pilings under one of these docks."

"Keep your head down and your powder dry, Commander," said Chief Burns when he got his mooring line back. He slowly backed his patrol boat away from ours and executed a sharp u-turn.

I nodded and then signaled for Taylor to take us over to the *Balboa Victory*.

After Chief Taylor killed all the navigation and interior lights on our patrol boat, he unbuckled the webbed belt from his waist and handed me his weapon. "You might need this, Commander," he said. "It's a Beretta .40 caliber, thirteen rounds in the magazine and there's one in the chamber so be careful. You have three spare clips of ammo and if the shooting starts, we'll be there before you're empty."

Taylor eased the patrol boat up to the ladder and I tested it with my full weight. "I'll go first." I said to Rachel.

Taylor leaned out the patrol boat's pilothouse window. "Take Sea Marshal Conway with you," he said. "He can guard the ladder while you search the ship."

"Good thinking," I said. "Thanks."

The ladder was made of heavy manila rope with hardwood rungs for steps and appeared to be fairly new. It was about twenty-five feet up to the main deck and as soon as I swung my legs over the ship's rail, I motioned for Rachel to start up the ladder. She had more trouble climbing the ladder than I did, there's a bit of an art to climbing a Jacob's ladder, and when she was on deck, Sea Marshal Conway scurried up the ladder with monkey-like quickness, his automatic rifle slung securely across his back.

When we were all aboard, Chief Taylor gave me thumbs up and then held two fingers to his eyes before pointing to me, his signal that he'd be watching us.

Right away, I noticed the escape hatch to the shaft alley was open and when we approached it, there were sounds coming from below. We listened and could occasionally hear muffled voices or metal on metal sounds.

"Somebody's down there," I whispered. "The question is who."

"Are we going down there?" Rachel asked.

"Not down the escape shaft," I said. "They'd hear us coming and could pick us off at will, we wouldn't have a chance. We'll try to sneak up on them through the engineroom."

Sea Marshal Conway was assigned to watch the shaft alley escape hatch and took up a position in the shadows of the *Balboa Victory's* poop deck.

The main deck doors to the accommodation space were all padlocked. Rachel and I searched for about ten minutes, climbed several steel stairways, and then finally found an aft facing door on the officer's deck that was unlocked and ajar. It was pitch black inside the ship and Rachel led the way, holding her hand over her flashlight lens, letting a small amount of light bleed through her fingers.

"I don't know where we're going," she said.

Staying close with my left hand on her shoulder, I whispered directions in her ear until we'd dropped down two decks and found a door to the engine room. The story Frank Burch told me this afternoon about his experience on the ship when it was in layup began playing through my mind.

Once inside the engine room, we found all the lights had been turned on so I took the lead, Rachel two steps behind me. We cautiously descended the engine room stairs past the boilers and the fireroom, listening for every faint sound. From time to time, we could hear someone talk or a dull metallic thud echo throughout the engine room. We paused at the main turbine, wondering which way to go. I decided to take the stairs at the forward end of the turbine, the afternoon tour of the *Dixie Victory* was still fresh in my mind and I had a sense of where I was going. Near the main condenser, I drew the weapon Chief Taylor gave me and checked to make sure there was a round in the chamber and that the safety was on.

Rachel and I stopped at the entrance to the shaft alley. The noises were louder and definitely coming from down the alleyway.

"If the shooting starts," I whispered. "Your only cover is going to be in the bilge."

Rachel grimaced as she looked into the filthy bilge but nodded acknowledgement. She drew her .357 magnum Colt Python from its holster and clutching it with both hands, she said, "Let's do it."

The electric bilge pump picked that moment to thunder to life, Rachel jumped at the sound, and the mechanical cacophony resonated throughout the engine room for about thirty seconds before subsiding.

"I hate this place," she said.

"At least the bilge is dry now."

"That makes me feel a whole lot better."

We were about twenty feet into the shaft alley when we saw somebody crawl out of the fuel tank inspection manhole on the left side of the shaft alley, the very same one where I noticed the fresh grease on the bolt threads. He was about sixty feet away. Black fuel oil smears coated his khaki coveralls and he wore a white towel or rag over his hair. Once clear of the manhole, he leaned over to retrieve something from a wooden box.

"Freeze, asshole," Rachel shouted as she forced her way by me on the narrow walkway.

The man said something unintelligible and began running down the walkway toward the vertical escape shaft.

Rachel had her weapon pointed at the man and I was afraid she was going to fire it. "Don't shoot down here," I screamed at her. "The bullets will ricochet."

Another head appeared from inside the manhole and when the man saw Rachel coming, he popped out of sight with gopher-like quickness. Rachel sprinted past the open fuel tank in pursuit of the escapee but stopped at the bottom of the escape shaft. Just as she started back toward me on the walkway, there was shouting followed by two rifle shots that reverberated down from the top of the escape shaft.

"I'm not coming in there after you," yelled Rachel into the open manhole. She scrunched her face when she got a whiff of the sulfurous stench emanating from the fuel oil tank where the men were hiding. "The police dog will be here in five minutes. Your friend just got shot trying to escape and you have two choices, come out and surrender with your hands up or wait until the police dog tears your asses into submission."

"You've got nowhere to go," I said into the black hole. "Make it easy on yourselves and give it up now."

It was only a few moments later when we heard a voice from inside the fuel tank say, "We're coming out, don't send the dog in."

"How many of you are in there?" Rachel asked.

"Four," said the voice. "Three now, Jeff's not in here anymore."

"Four total?" she asked. "And there's still three inside?"

"Yes, we're coming out. Is the dog out there?"

"Not yet, but you better get your asses out here."

The first one out was a kid about nineteen, dressed in coveralls and wearing a rag on his head like the one that had run away. I moved back on the walkway and made him sit cross-legged with his hands on his head. The second one out was another youth dressed like the other two and when he came out, he saw his friend sitting on the walkway so he quietly assumed the same position. The third youth crawled out of the fuel tank and started to sit with the others.

"Wait, I know you!" Rachel said as she pulled the rag from his head. "You're Ben Short!"

23

"You're Ben Short, we found your fingerprints in James Wierman's car," Rachel said to the youth that had just exited the fuel oil tank in the shaft alley of the *Balboa Victory*. "You told us he let you use his car to go to the hardware store."

Ben Short didn't say a word to Rachel as he assumed the position with his companions on the rusty deck plates. I squeezed past her on the walkway and moved to the end of the shaft alley. I stood at the bottom of the escape trunk and yelled up to Sea Marshal Conway several times but got no response. Maybe he had the escaped suspect in custody and was out of earshot of the hatch opening. I began to worry that maybe there were others aboard ship that we hadn't seen and Conway was the victim of the two shots we'd heard.

"Jared, you've got to see this." Rachel was probing the inside of the opened fuel tank with her flashlight.

Rachel handed me her flashlight and I knelt to examine the inside of the tank. The black-oil coated fuel reservoir gobbled up the small amount of illumination the flashlight was providing, but slowly my eyes adjusted to the dim interior and I could see heaps of brick-sized silver bars stacked inside. A mound of the bars was just inside the manhole and I grabbed one, surprised at how heavy it was for its size. As I was bringing it out of the manhole, I could hear boots coming down the steel ladder in the shaft alley escape trunk. The silver bar dropped to the steel walkway with a metallic clang and I noticed that the silver paint had been scraped away in one corner to reveal the gold underneath.

"Drop your weapons and step back," said the voice.

"San Pedro Police," Rachel yelled.

"Drop your weapons and step back," repeated the voice from behind me on the walkway. I turned to face a man, dressed in black, that was pointing a Colt AR-15 assault rifle at my face. There were three more men dressed in black on the walkway behind him.

"Coast Guard," I said.

"Sir, drop your weapon and step away from it," said the man with the rifle. "We're with the U.S. Treasury Department, don't make me shoot you!"

Boots thundered on the steel walkway coming from the direction of the engine room. I saw four more men dressed in black converging on us.

"I'm with the San Pedro Police," Rachel protested. "This is our bust."

"Drop your weapon, officer," the Treasury Agent said. "We'll sort through all this in a minute, but right now, I need for you two to drop your weapons."

Rachel and I laid our firearms on the walkway and the men in black escorted us to the engine room where we were placed under armed guard on the steel floorplates near the main condenser.

"Those are the kids from Cabrillo Vo-Tech," Rachel said softly, looking at our guard out of the corner of her eye.

"And I'll bet that's the gold that didn't go to the bottom of the South China Sea with the *SeaTrans Expeditor.*"

Rachel nodded.

"No talking," said our guard, his Colt AR-15 at the ready.

It was about ten o'clock when Lieutenant Richards showed up with the senior U.S. Treasury Agent on the scene.

"She's one of mine," Lieutenant Richards said. "And this is Commander Jared Stanton of the U.S. Coast Guard."

"Commander Stanton, I'll explain to you like I explained to Lieutenant Richards here," said the senior Treasury Agent who was fully outfitted in neatly pressed SWAT gear. "This matter concerns neither the San Pedro Police Department nor the Coast Guard, it's a matter for the Treasury Department. We have jurisdiction here and want you off the scene immediately."

"I'd like my weapon back," I said.

"You request has been noted, Commander. You need to leave the scene." He nodded at our guard. "Escort these people off the vessel."

"Damn it Terazzo," Lieutenant Richards said as we climbed out of the engine room. "I told you we were off the case. What the hell are you doing down here tonight?"

Rachel shrugged. "It's my last night."

"You ain't shittin' it's your last night!"

***

On my way home, I stopped by the gas station mini-mart on the corner of Pacific Avenue and 8th Street to pick up a few things. The prices were outrageous and I only had a single twenty-dollar bill left, so I limited myself to a quart of milk, two cans of Red Bull for tomorrow morning, a loaf of bread, and some already questionable looking lunchmeat.

Once we'd cleared the *Balboa Victory* and were in the parking lot, Lieutenant Richards had briefed us on the status of the case. He explained that as soon as traces of gold were found on Wierman's knife, the U.S. Treasury Department showed up and took over the investigation on James Wierman's murder but that he was under strict orders from his superiors to keep it quiet because the case was ongoing. Fingerprints lifted from the Cadillac Escalade at the scene of Fat Louie's murder led to a Vietnamese gang in Little Saigon out near Westminster. Fat Louie's pawnshop records showed he frequently moved jewelry, probably when he suspected it was stolen, through a gold and gem broker named Nikkei Dhe in Little Saigon.

"It looks like those Vo-Tech kids got into it with James Wierman when they found the gold, then things got a little too rough when it didn't turn out like they planned, probably because Wierman wanted to report what he'd found. Once they killed Wierman, they needed to fence the gold on the fly and went to Fat Louie to do it," Lieutenant Richards told us. "But when Nikkei Dhe found out what Fat Louie was sitting on, he sent his thugs to lean on poor old Louie with the intention of cutting him out of the deal and stealing all the gold. Too bad Fat Louie didn't have the gold yet. There really is no such thing as honor among thieves."

Milk washed down another batch of Rachel's headache pills as I pulled onto Pacific Avenue to head home. I constantly checked my rearview mirror more out of habit than paranoia. It all made sense to me now. The Treasury Department had more than ten billion dollars worth of gold floating around somewhere that they needed to get back in Fort Knox before some smart-ass citizens group found out it was missing and started raising hell. The public doesn't have much faith in the government as it is, but the Vietnamese gold fiasco would send shock waves through the political scene even today. Maybe Nixon had originally authorized using Fort Knox gold to fight a mercenary war in Southeast Asia, but every elected official and Treasury bureaucrat with knowledge of the incident since Vietnam would have their heads on the chopping block for it. Just because you inherited the skeleton in the closet, doesn't mean you won't have a lot of explaining to do once somebody finds it there.

There was a Jeep Wrangler and a Mitsubishi Eclipse occupying each of my parking spaces and I was forced to leave the garage and park on the street. The Reynoza brothers were getting a little out of hand with the parking situation and I vowed to talk with them this weekend.

A Friday night party threatened to explode into the hallway from the Reynoza's apartment so I just walked on by instead of confronting them. It might be Sunday afternoon until they were coherent enough to hold a rational conversation.

The small bag of groceries from the mini-mart was cradled in my left arm while I unlocked my apartment, and bumping the door open with my hip, I reached for the light switch. Suddenly, I was flying forward, being propelled by the hand clutching my shirt. A solid blow to my right ear sent me to the floor.

The blonde surfer from the *Balboa Victory*'s cargo hold closed the door while the black one with dreadlocks stood over me.

"You gotta' quit doing that," I said, starting to sit up. "It hurts like hell."

Dreadlocks kicked me in the chest.

"You assholes need to learn some people skills," I said. "That's not even necessary. Maybe you haven't heard that the case is closed."

"Where is it?" Dreadlocks asked.

"It's in one of the fuel tanks on the *Balboa Victory*," I said, starting to sit up again. "Down in the shaft alley. The Treasury Department has the gold back, the case is closed."

Dreadlocks kicked me again. "Not the gold, dumbass. The notebook."

Before I knew it, Blondie had me on my feet and into a kitchen chair where he zip-tied my hands behind my back.

Dreadlocks backhanded me across the face. "Make this as hard on yourself as you want," he said. "Where's the notebook?"

I could taste blood in my mouth, the salty-sweet tang stinging my tongue, but I forced a laugh. I could feel my nose bleeding. "There's nothing in the notebook."

Dreadlocks hit me again. Harder.

"Quit doing that," I said, spitting blood on the floor. "There's nothing in the notebook and the gold is going back where it belongs."

Blondie stepped in front of me, holding up a syringe and a glass vial for me to see.

Dreadlocks' cell phone rang and he stepped inside my bedroom and closed the door.

"We're going to get the notebook one way or another," Blondie said, exhibiting the syringe, a sneer plastered across his face. "I prefer to use less violent methods but creative methods. My partner on the other hand..."

"We've got the girl," Dreadlocks said, coming back from the bedroom. "The boss wants us over there right away."

"What do we do with him?" Blondie asked.

"Leave him here for now. If the girl doesn't have the notebook, then he does."

Blondie added more zip-ties to my hands and feet and then said, "I'll give him a little of this to keep him quiet until we get back."

Dreadlocks held my head to the side while Blondie injected a healthy dose from the vial into my jugular vein. Immediately, white heat rushed through my brain and the sound inside my head was just like I was standing between two passing freight trains.

"You guys are CIA," I stammered, my head too heavy to hold up. "You're not supposed to be operating domestically."

Dreadlocks held me by my hair and put his face in mine. "You have two problems, Commander," he said. "First of all, you don't know who we are. Secondly, even if think you know who we are, we're officially seven thousand miles from here right now. So I'm going to ask you once more. Where's the notebook?"

The white heat had moved from my head to my chest and with each heartbeat, it traveled farther down my arms and legs, searing my insides as it went.

"There's no notebook, it was a bluff."

Dreadlocks let my head fall, stood back, and backhanded me again, the blow knocking the chair over and I smacked the side of my head as I crashed to the floor.

"We really need to have a serious talk, Commander," Dreadlocks said. "You better hope we get want we want from the girl."

24

The beach was hotter than hell, I was sweating like a pig, and my mouth felt like a thousand camels had walked through it, everyone of them stopping to crap on my tongue. Rachel Terazzo walked down the beach holding the black notebook and smiling at me. Suddenly she opened it and red scorpions fell out. "Watch this," she said, climbing inside. When she disappeared, the notebook slammed closed and tumbled to the ground, lying motionless, starkly contrasted by the crystal white sand of the beach. Surprisingly, the sand felt cool on my left cheek and ear. Hard but cool.

The freight train sounds had just started to disappear when I heard a key slipping into the lock and my apartment door opening.

"Dude, are you okay?"

"We gotta' stop meeting like this, Julio."

Julio Reynoza rushed past me and into the kitchen.

"Hold still, dude, I don't want to cut you," he said, kneeling next to me.

The zip-ties dug deeper into my wrists just before I felt them release. Julio moved to cut my ankles free with the Ginzu steak knife.

"What happened?"

"I need something to drink." My hands and feet still felt like they were on fire.

"You want a beer?"

"Water. Cold water."

Julio Reynoza helped me to my feet and the trains began roaring in my head again. Bill Baldwin, the apartment complex manager, was standing just inside my front door looking slack-jawed and dumbstruck.

"Sharon was coming back with pizza and she recognized the black dude coming out of your apartment," Julio said. "He was the same guy she saw the other night down in the garage, the guy with the funny hair."

The floor in my apartment was moving like the deck of a ship at sea and I timed the rolling so I could get to the kitchen sink. I fumbled with the faucet and when the water finally felt cold, I drank straight from the tap in huge gulps. When I had my fill, I cupped both hands under the running water and then rinsed my face.

"Sharon told me she saw those guys coming out of your apartment, I knocked on your door but you didn't answer so I got Bill to open it up," Julio said. "Who were those guys? Are you okay?"

My head was too heavy to hold up and I was short of breath. My apartment started a slow counterclockwise spin as Julio helped me to the table to sit down.

The door to my apartment closed and when I looked up, Bill Baldwin was gone.

"Dude, you're in some shit," Julio said. "What's going on? Who were those guys and why do they keep knocking the shit out of you? Your neck's bleeding."

Rachel. Dreadlocks said they had the girl. He meant Rachel.

"Is he all right?" asked the leggy blonde in cutoffs and tube top who was leaning against my refrigerator while she nonchalantly ate a piece of pizza. "He doesn't look so good."

It seemed like an eternity until I could find Lieutenant Richard's phone number on my cell phone. It took a little longer to focus on the screen and buttons so I could make the call.

"They have Rachel," I said when he answered.

"Who is this?"

"Jared Stanton."

"How do you know they have her?"

"They were just in my apartment and I heard them say they had her."

"Her patrol unit was rear-ended at a stoplight on Harbor Boulevard a half-hour ago, when she got out of her car to confront them, they abducted her at gunpoint."

"We've got to get her back."

"There were witnesses and we've got a vehicle description to go with a plate number. We'll get her back. Why were they at your apartment, Commander?"

"They're looking for a notebook that Brooke Wierman gave us."

"What's in the notebook?"

"Nothing."

"Nothing?"

"Yeah, but they don't know that."

"Who are these guys?"

"Do you remember the two CIA agents that were in the *Balboa Victory's* cargo hold the night we found Wierman's body?"

"I remember them."

"That's who you're looking for."

There was a pause and then Lieutenant Richards asked, "What the fuck is going on, Commander? Why would the CIA grab Rachel? What aren't you telling me?"

"I'm not sure what's going on and I'm telling you everything I know," I said. "I thought they were looking for the gold, but now they want the notebook, so James Wierman must have had something else that they still want to get their hands on."

"I've gotta' take another call," Lieutenant Richards said. "But I'm sending a car over to your place right now. Don't worry, we'll get her back."

The trains in my head and the heat were gone now. Whatever Blondie had injected into my bloodstream was wearing off, leaving a dull fog in my brain. Why did they want that notebook? What were they afraid of? The jury was still out, but it was beginning to look like the CIA hadn't killed James Wierman or Fat Louie, but they sure as hell knocked me around a couple of times and now they'd kidnapped Rachel. All over an old confession letter and then a notebook with nothing in it.

Maybe it was the drugs Blondie gave me that slowed my brain down, or maybe I'd just been over-thinking it all along, but suddenly it hit me like a ton of bricks. Rachel accidentally said it. Her words rang as clear and true as if she were standing right next to me. And Beverly Cristy was right. Lloyd Waller's words at lunch jelled with what the stranger said at the fireboat station. None of it had made much sense at the time, but now I knew how to find Rachel. If it wasn't already too late.

The ten-millimeter Glock had been my service weapon when I was with the Bureau and was stowed in a Florsheim shoebox in my closet.

"Where're you going?" Julio asked. Sharon stood next to him, barefoot, eating another slice of pizza, a small dab of red sauce on the end of nose.

"To look for the shit," I said. "And to put an end to it."

25

The air in San Pedro was eerily still without even a hint of breeze off the Pacific. I'd been in Oklahoma for training with the Bureau when a series of tornadoes rolled through the area. Just before they hit, the air was so thick and humid I needed gills to breathe and it was so quiet that I could hear myself sweat. Tonight was like that, and I was so pumped up right now that even my eyelids were sweating.

Switching the headlights off, I eased the government sedan between two shipping containers at the China Lines freight yard across the street from the Harbor Light, my heartbeat pounding in my ears. My right eye began an annoying twitch and my fingers trembled on the steering wheel. Was it the drugs Blondie gave me, Rachel's pills, or was it my own adrenaline making me shake and sweat? Hell, for all I knew, my heart was ready to explode from all the chemicals I had in my bloodstream tonight.

It was just past eleven-thirty and the traffic had all but died on the street. Reverend Johnny was still on his corner in front of the hotel, pacing and looking nervous. I waited. But I didn't have to wait for long.

Johnny grabbed his shopping cart and disappeared around the corner and up 4th Street. Racing through the container yard without headlights, I shot out the security gate, took a right on Harbor Boulevard and a quick left onto 4th Street. Reverend Johnny had crossed the street and was a block and a half ahead of me. I eased up the street without headlights, staying next to the curb and keeping my distance, controlling my speed with the emergency brake so my brake lights wouldn't come on.

Reverend Johnny stopped, looked around, and then ducked into an alley with his shopping cart. With the motor still running and the car in park, I slumped down in the front seat, out of view, keeping an eye on the alley Johnny had ducked into.

In about three minutes, a white Jaguar sedan stopped at the intersection ahead, paused for a moment, and then made a right turn onto 4th Street, coming to a halt in front of Johnny's alley. When the Jaguar's right rear door opened to let Johnny in, the dome lights illuminated two other men inside but I couldn't identify them.

After the Jaguar sped off and made a left turn onto Pacific Avenue, I floored the accelerator to catch up.   Waiting until a steel-gray Dodge minivan came down the street from the right, I punched the gas pedal to the floor and dropped in behind him, only turning on my headlights when the minivan was between the Jaguar and me. The minivan and the Jaguar went right on 25th Street, drove to the top of San Pedro Hill, and then headed north until 25th merged with Palos Verde Drive. The minivan I was using as a shield made a right turn two miles later at Hawthorne Boulevard so I had to adjust my speed accordingly.   Palos Verde Drive turned into an unlit two-lane road after Hawthorne Boulevard and the driver of the Jaguar would be watching his rearview mirror to make sure nobody was following him.   As we approached Portuguese Bend, the Jaguar slowed without using his brakes and I knew he was testing me. I ran up on the Jaguar at the speed limit but signaled right and turned off on a residential side street. A hundred yards up the side street, I killed my headlights, made a hard u-turn, and got back on Palos Verde Drive in time to see the Jaguar's taillights disappear around a bend.

I sped along Palos Verde Drive with my headlights off as it wound north through an area of upscale Old-California Spanish style homes with million dollar views of the Pacific Ocean and the Channel Islands. Driving without headlights was treacherous, but by noting where the Jaguar rounded the curves and feeling the shoulder with my right front tire, a technique I'd honed at the

FBI Academy, I was able to keep up. Near Punta Bonita, a small peninsula known for its mansion size homes and close proximity to the migration route of Pacific whales transiting between Mexico and Alaska, the Jaguar turned left and headed towards the ocean. The narrow Sycamore lined road dropped off toward the Pacific and with my window down, I could hear the surf and smell the seaspray. At the end of the road, the Jaguar pulled into a large circular driveway of a brightly lit three-story marble estate perched on the bluffs overlooking the ocean.   Standing on my emergency brake pedal until I thought the cable would snap, the government sedan labored to a halt about a hundred yards from the mansion.

I'd never been here before, but I recognized the mansion because I'd seen it on television. It was Franklin Sheridan's humble abode.

My fingers were trembling on the steering wheel as I watched the three men exit the Jaguar and disappear through one of the massive double front doors. I really needed one of my pills to calm my nerves but I knew my mouth was too dry to swallow it.

Beverly Cristy was right. Reverend Johnny was a fake.

The Glock was on the front seat next to my cell phone and I checked to make sure a round was chambered. Should I call Lieutenant Richards and tell him where I was? How long would it take to explain to him what I knew? Would he think I was crazy because I'd followed a homeless guy to Franklin Sheridan's mansion? What if they were holding Rachel somewhere else?   I hadn't actually seen her yet. Would they really bring her here? If Rachel wasn't here right now, but someplace else, like a warehouse in San Pedro, a knock on the front door would be her death sentence. If I did call Lieutenant Richards, we couldn't get inside the mansion without a search warrant that might take hours to obtain and then a confrontation would only tip them off. Maybe I could get past the mansion's security system to see if Rachel was really inside. As soon as I knew for sure where they had her, I could call Lieutenant Richards and have him swarm the place with a SWAT team. My mouth was dry, the scar on my jaw itched like crazy, and I still had a million questions.

Unfortunately, the answer to my questions came in the form of an ice cold steel barrel that was being pressed into my left ear. "Real slow," said the voice outside my window. "Hand me the weapon or they'll be picking up your brains with a stick and a spoon."

26

The inside of the mansion was gorgeous and I would have liked to visit it sometime under more favorable circumstances.   Underneath my feet was the finest Italian marble, and two staircases, one on each side of the entryway, spiraled gracefully upward toward the next two floors. Hand-woven oriental rugs adorned the marble floor and exquisite chandeliers hung midway to the floor from the ceiling two stories above. Opposite the entryway, on the main floor, was an expansive great room with floor to ceiling windows offering a view of the ocean and surf battered cliffs below.   The great room had twin grand pianos and several separate sitting areas decorated with French provincial furniture and delicate tapestries.

The gun was out of my ear and squarely between my shoulder blades now.   The gun's owner I recognized as one of the jugglers that had been on the sidewalk near Pacific Pawn and Loan the day Rachel and I talked to Fat Louie. I had a bad feeling about where things were going next.

The door to my right opened and Blondie stepped out. "What a pleasant surprise, Commander Stanton," he said. "We were just talking about how to get you over here. That party going on down the hall from your apartment is very inconvenient and Detective Terazzo is being less than cooperative."

Blondie motioned me through the door and the gun nudged my spine from behind. Inside the door off the entryway was a large office with a magnificent African mahogany desk and matching bookcases lining the wall. Leather settees were scattered around the office and the faces in the room were familiar. So was the smoke from the Cuban cigars. Cohibas. Reverend Johnny was sitting in a European wingback armchair to my right and the juggler's partner from outside Fat Louie's pawnshop sat with Dreadlocks in a pair of armchairs across the desk from Malcolm Cross.

The Cohiba smoking stranger from the Balboa Victory's parking lot stood next to the five-foot high marble fireplace that had a live fire going. No fake flames or natural gas for Franklin Sheridan's mansion. Of all the strange thoughts to enter my brain at the time, I wondered how they got approved to have a fireplace with all the air quality restrictions in place in the Los Angeles basin these days. I guess the rich can do whatever they want.

"I tried to tell you to go home the other night, Commander," said the stranger as he blew cigar smoke in my direction. "But you wouldn't fucking listen."

Malcolm Cross had his elbows on the desk, looking over his hands, his fingers spread wide, and the fingertips on his right hand touching the corresponding fingertips on the left hand like he was praying.

"I can't tell you how sorry I am to see you here, Commander Stanton," he said, sighing over his hands. "It indicates to me that you have things figured out, and that bodes ill for you."

"I can't say I'm all that happy to see you either, Mr. Cross," I said. "But then again, maybe I should call you Captain Bailey of the Navy SEALS, or maybe even Admiral Greenwalt from Naval Intelligence."

"See," Malcolm Cross said, gesturing to the others in the room. "Commander Stanton did figure it out."

The office door closed behind me.

"I see you've taken over Mr. Sheridan's house as well as his office," I said.

"Frank won't be returning here, he's much too ill," Malcolm Cross said. "He was a fine businessman, he did well with the money I invested in SeaTrans, but money doesn't buy everything, and even the finest doctors won't extend Frank's life much longer."

"The Treasury Department has your gold," I said.

Malcolm Cross rose from behind the desk and waved nonchalantly in the air. "More specifically, Commander Stanton, they have recovered what little actually remains of the gold. But that's neither here nor there," he said. "It's a write-off, a lost asset. Nothing more. The bulk of the gold was invested in SeaTrans long ago."

"James Wierman recognized you, didn't he?" I said.

"That was most unfortunate," Malcolm Cross said. "But after so many years and thousands of names and faces, I can't be faulted for not remembering just one name."

"But James Wierman remembered."

"Maybe, after a while. But even that situation was manageable."

"It got him killed."

"No, it was the Treasury Department that got him killed," Malcolm Cross said.

"The Treasury Department?" I asked. "How were they responsible."

Malcolm Cross began to pace the office floor, pausing briefly to look into the fire before turning back to me. "You would think one department in the government would know what another department was doing and maybe offer a little cooperation," he said. "It just isn't so. The Central Intelligence Agency is still contracting us for work that is strictly confidential, but then the Internal Revenue Service comes knocking on the door to collect taxes for something that never officially happened. The Treasury Department wouldn't let go of the gold, even though the CIA had long ago written the incident off as a loss. They put one of their agents in the layup fleet as a security guard, like I wouldn't know who he was, and we couldn't remove the gold. Our only choice was to bring the ship down here where we could monitor it."

"Why didn't you just give them their gold back?"

"It was too late for that, Commander. Most of the gold is gone and besides, they wanted more than the gold. They wanted me," Malcolm Cross said. "Some sort of silly idea about bringing me to justice."

"What a silly idea," I said.

"After all I've done for this country over the last thirty years. They wanted to send me to jail."

"You stole ten million ounces of gold that belonged to the people of the United States."

"Gold that was already being used illegally. Is it a crime if a thief steals from a thief? Does a drug addict complain to the police when his dealer cheats him?" Malcolm Cross said. "That gold was nothing more that startup capital and so much good has come from it."

"Right," I said.

"That gold was used to keep this nation safe for over thirty years," Malcolm Cross said.

"The end justifies the means."

"This is the real world, Commander," Malcolm Cross said. "Not some children's fairy tale where everything is black and white, where good always triumphs over evil. This country has a hell of a fight on its hands and I'm here to make sure we don't lose that fight."

"Save the lecture, I've heard it before," I said. "Somebody has to do the dirty work, fight evil with evil. You do the dirty work and the CIA gets to keep their squeaky clean image. How convenient."

"Your idealism is quaint, Commander."

"I'm surprised the CIA continued to deal with you after you stole their gold."

Malcolm Cross laughed and shook his head. "The CIA hires the best. They wanted me on their side because they didn't want me working against them."

"You were supposed to help the CIA move the gold once it reached Vietnam, but instead, you intercepted it and made it look like the ship went to the bottom of the South China Sea."

"The CIA operation was being run by idiots," Malcolm Cross said. "I took the gold shipment right from under their noses... and they never even knew it was gone. It was a cheap lesson in reality for them. They got better and stronger because of what I did to them."

The side door to the study opened and Rachel Terazzo was shoved into the room. Her face was bruised and swollen, blood oozed from her mouth and nose, her clothes torn and disheveled. I could only imagine what they'd done to her. When she saw me her eyes widened and I could see she wanted to cry but stifled it.

"She won't give it up," said a bearded gray-haired man I'd never seen before.

"Screw you!" Rachel said to everyone in the room. "I mailed the notebook to the Treasury Department just like James Wierman wanted us to. You assholes are finished!"

"Rachel," I said. "Tell them the truth, tell them there was nothing in the notebook and it was just a ploy to find out who beat me up in the garage."

Beneath her bruised and swollen face, I could see Rachel was conflicted. If it were up to her, she would die before she told them the truth. It was in her eyes. But now that I was here, she didn't know what to do.

"Maybe Commander Stanton can get her to tell us where the notebook is," Malcolm Cross said, motioning to Dreadlocks.

Dreadlocks stood up and faced me.

"Just out of curiosity, Mr. Cross," I said. "What were you looking for in James Wierman's house the night he got killed?"

"The same thing we're looking for now," he said. "Information. We had to be ahead of the police investigation into his murder to make sure he didn't posses any incriminating information that would jeopardize our current covert operations. I couldn't take a chance that he recognized me, the field action at his home was simply routine damage control and risk assessment."

"What did you take from his office?" I asked.

"That was a little souvenir I took for myself," he said. "Wierman had a picture of the *SeaTrans Expeditor* on his wall and I couldn't resist. That little operation made us what we are today." Malcolm Cross motioned to Dreadlocks again.

Dreadlocks smiled as he stood up and withdrew a folding knife from his pocket. "Where shall we start, Commander?" he asked. "A finger?

A toe? Or should we just get it over with and start with the genitals?"

There was no doubt in my mind that Rachel and I would soon be dead if we didn't do something. My math had it seven against two, and Rachel wasn't in shape to do much of anything right now. She might be able to take the old guy that brought her in, but that left me to face the other six by myself and they were all government trained assassins. I tried to catch Rachel's eye, if one of us could jump Malcolm Cross, we might stand a chance.

I spun and made a move for the gun in my back but missed it. Instead I caught a short left hook just below my right ear that sent me to the floor.

The Cohiba smoking asshole laughed. "Nice move, Commander." He shook his head as he puffed on his cigar.

"Get up," Malcolm Cross said.

I got to my feet and considered rushing Malcolm Cross but he was too far away. I'd have a bullet through the back of my skull before I ever reached him.

Dreadlocks approached me and held the knife up for me to see.

"Well, Rachel," Malcolm Cross said. "Your own pain means nothing to you. Let's see how much of Commander Stanton's pain you can stand to watch."

Dreadlocks smiled again. He stood so close I could feel him breathing on me and then he held the knife next to my right eye.

I wasn't in the mood to be tortured. If I was going to die, I was going to go down fighting. I spit in Dreadlocks' face and when he went to wipe it away, I grabbed the knife and threw my weight into him. We fell to the floor with a thud. I had both hands on the knife but Dreadlocks was stronger than I was. A boot kicked me in the head and I rolled over as best I could to get away from it. Dreadlocks pinned me on my back and then the Cohiba smoking stranger walked over and knelt next to us on the floor. He forcefully pried the knife away from both our hands.

"Boys, we're not on the playground," the cigar smoker said. "Get up."

"This is all very entertaining, Commander," Malcolm Cross said. "All I want is the notebook."

"We're dead anyway," I said. "Maybe you should worry about what Rachel really did with it."

I was helped to my feet by hands from behind me and as soon as I had a chance, I landed a solid right hand to Dreadlocks' left ear. I was promptly grabbed from behind and restrained again.

"You asshole," Dreadlocks said, and then he had another knife.

White thunder exploded in the room, the concussion pounding my eardrums. Dreadlocks stumbled, grabbing his upper left thigh that was gushing blood between his fingers, and then he hit the floor with a thud.

"U.S. Treasury," Reverend Johnny yelled. "Who's next?"

Rachel dropped to her knees. Reverend Johnny gave me a handgun from somewhere.

"If they move, shoot them, Commander," Reverend Johnny said, flipping his cell phone open with one hand, an automatic pistol in the other. "Back-up is two minutes away."

Malcolm Cross shook his head. "My instincts were right about you, Johnny," he said. "I never trusted you, but you fooled everyone else."

"Shut up," Reverend Johnny said.

"You'll destroy one of freedom's vital assets. This country can't survive without people like us," Malcolm Cross said. "Put down the gun, Johnny, it's not too late."

Reverend Johnny looked at his watch and then walked over to Malcolm Cross. "U.S. Treasury Agent, put down your weapon and step away," Reverend Johnny said. And then he shot Malcolm Cross between the eyes.

I staggered back as Malcolm Cross crumpled to the floor, blood flowing from his forehead, forming a sticky crimson pool on the marble. Reverend Johnny placed a handgun next to the body.

"Those were my orders, Commander," Reverend Johnny said. "He'd gone too far over the line and was working both sides of the street. SeaTrans provided a cover for his little black-ops group that contracted with the CIA, but then he began working for any foreign government with cash. He lost his way."

"What about them?" I asked, gesturing to the others in the room. "They all saw what happened."

"They'll have their chance to come back to our side," Reverend Johnny said. "They'll be debriefed and offered reorientation training."

"And if they don't?   If they try to testify against you?"

"They'll spend the rest of their lives living in a six by eight foot cell a thousand feet below the Nevada desert. There really is only one option for them. This is a matter of national security."

I knelt next to Rachel and put an arm around her shoulder. She buried her face in my chest.

The Cohiba smoking stranger threw his cigar into the fireplace. "Why didn't you just stay out of it?"

The room filled with men dressed in black SWAT gear.

"He resisted," Reverend Johnny said.

"Good work, agent," said the man I'd seen on the *Balboa Victory* with Lieutenant Richards less than two hours ago. "Good work."

27

It had been twelve days since I watched Reverend Johnny terminate Malcolm Cross at Franklin Sheridan's mansion on Punta Bonita. Since then the summer heat had settled over San Pedro Harbor like a vile plague. A weak high-pressure system over the eastern desert was responsible for stifling the Pacific Ocean's cool sea breezes for the last week.

Lieutenant Richards and I attended James Wierman's funeral and later took his widow and daughter aside to explain the outcome of our investigations. Officially, James Wierman's cause of death proved to be natural causes, more specifically, heart failure. Two Vo-Tech students had tried to help him out of the engineroom when he first became ill, but panicked and ran when he died in the cargo hold. They both had police records and were afraid they would somehow be blamed for his death. The Wierman's home invasion was just one of a string of similar such crimes in the area and was still under investigation. It was a pretty bad lie, but it was one the Treasury Department had given us to tell.

I wasn't sure where the four Cabrillo Vo-Tech students we caught trying to remove the gold from the *Balboa Victory* ended up. The Treasury Department took them into custody and they might be in Guantanamo Bay for all I knew. I wasn't sure how the Treasury people planned to keep the students from talking about the gold, but I suspect that a few nights behind bars as some big hairy pervert's girlfriend would have them agreeing to just about anything else.

My dreams about Elisha had given way to nightmares about the execution of Malcolm Cross and the torture of Fat Louie. The way I saw it, I only had two choices. The first was the coward's way out by continuing the pills. The other was to get off the pills altogether, but that was a lot scarier.

My shrink had been calling because I hadn't been to see him in over three weeks. I was burned out by all the touchy-feely therapy sessions with him and hadn't returned any of his calls. Besides, if I told him about the nightmares I was having now, I might end up living in a tiny holding cell beneath the Nevada desert.

"It's hotter than a twenty-dollar whore out there today," said Stan as he pushed a mug of cold draft beer across the bar.

There wasn't much foam on the beer but it was cold and the mug was frosty. I'd quit the whiskey a week ago and was down to just two pills a day. The pill count showed they would run out in twenty-two days so I still had some time to live in denial.

"You're not as interesting since you quit drinking," Stan said.

"That's what people are saying."

"Are you having something to eat?"

"Cajun prime rib, right?" I asked.

Stan nodded. "How do you want it done?"

"Kill the E-Coli."

What haunted me most was that Malcolm Cross was right. There's always dirty work that needs to get done and nobody wants to do it. Migrant farm workers harvest our food, maids clean our toilets, and young children toil in factories overseas making shoes and clothes under horrible conditions so we can maintain our level of comfort. We walk from air conditioned buildings to air conditioned cars, pop pre-packaged food bought at the super market into the microwave, and then sit down in our living rooms to watch reality shows on television. How ridiculous is that? We wouldn't know what reality was if it bit us in the ass, and it was people like Malcolm Cross that made sure we never would.

Reverend Johnny said Malcolm Cross had gone too far. I'd thought about that a lot in the last twelve days. Just exactly where do you draw the line for something like that? What is too far and how do you know when you get there? I sure as shit had screwed it up in Boca Raton.

Stan slid another beer across the bar. "That guy wants to buy you a beer."

I looked up to acknowledge the man at the other end of the bar that was dressed in tan slacks and a light blue golf shirt. He came down and took a seat next to me.

"You don't recognize me, do you?"

"Nope."

"I'm being reassigned and just wanted to say goodbye. I'll miss this place."

"Reverend Johnny?"

Johnny had shaved his beard, cut his hair, and looked completely different now. He held a finger to his lips and nodded at Stan.

"I've been undercover here for five years and I kind of got used to this place. I'll miss it," Reverend Johnny said quietly. "I've been watching you sit in this bar ever since you came to town."

"You were undercover on Malcolm Cross for five years?"

"He was pretty cautious, it took awhile to infiltrate his organization," Reverend Johnny said. "But he recruited exclusively from government agencies and I'd been with the Secret Service."

"That's a long time to be on an undercover assignment," I said. "How'd you do it?"

"You do what you have to do. We knew he had the gold, we just didn't know where it was." Reverend Johnny smiled at me. "A lot of these street people you see are really working for one government agency or another. They're invisible to the average person, as a matter of fact, people try real hard not to look at them at all, so it works out pretty good."

"So what are they really doing?"

"This and that. Watching. Collecting information. There are a lot of things going on in a place like San Pedro that nobody knows about. Not even you."

"Anything you want to tell me about?"

"We'll let you know if something comes up."

For a brief moment, I had the urge to press the issue, but quickly decided to wash the thought down with a sip of cold flat beer. Sometimes there are things you just don't want to know about.

"By the way, thanks for your help at Punta Bonita. I really owe you," I said. "You know, if you hadn't bought me a beer and come over, I never would have recognized you."

Reverend Johnny smiled again. "You always put money in my coffee can. Not a lot of people treat others like you do."

I shrugged and toyed with my beer.

"Can I offer you some advice?" he said. "As someone that's spent a lot of time working undercover."

"Sure."

"Like I said, I've been watching you since you got to town, and of course I know all about what happened to you in Boca Raton."

"I thought you had advice."

"I do," Reverend Johnny said. "It's really hard to keep your head screwed on straight when you're working undercover."

"No shit."

"We do things we wouldn't normally do and it's just a part of the job," he said. "You can drive yourself crazy wondering if you did the right thing. My advice is that you don't worry about the morality of what you have to do, that responsibility belongs to whoever gave you the assignment."

The image of Malcolm Cross with a bullet hole in his forehead flashed through my mind. "How do you not worry about the morality of what happened at Punta Bonita?"

"Both you and Detective Terazzo should be dead," he said. "Malcolm Cross intended to kill you and he wouldn't have even blinked an eye."

Reverend Johnny finished his beer and stood up to leave. "You have to forgive yourself," he said, putting a hand on my shoulder. "Nobody's on this earth one day longer than they're supposed to be. God makes sure of that. Fate is out of our hands and we have to learn to forgive ourselves today or we'll never be able to function tomorrow. You should be dead now, but you're not. Make a fresh start. It's time."

Nursing my beer, I considered Reverend Johnny's parting words. How do you forgive yourself when you walk up and shoot somebody between the eyes? How could I possibly forgive myself for what I'd done to Elisha?

The Cajun prime rib sandwich was spicier than usual and I wondered if it had always been that way and my taste buds were just more sensitive since I'd quit the whiskey. My cell phone rang and I wiped my hands before I answered it.

"Commander Stanton," said Chief Burns. "We have a situation on a vessel out at the San Pedro breakwater."

"What kind of situation?"

"The M.V. Reposa, sir," Chief Burns said. "She's the Argentine freighter that had a cargo manifest discrepancy."

"What about it?"

"Sir, we found weapons."

"What kind of weapons?"

"You better take a look."

"Pick me up at Berth 68 in ten minutes."

"Yes, sir," Chief Burns said.

I was waiting for Stan to bring my credit card back when Rachel slipped onto the stool next to me.

"You're predictable," she said.

"How about that?" I said. "I tried calling you."

"When?"

"Several times. Your cell phone was turned off and I left a couple of notes on your door."

"I've been busy," she said and then she held up her badge. "I'm back to work now."

"I thought you had the trial coming up."

"They copped a plea."

"Really?"

"Turns out those scumbags were wanted for the same thing in Texas. They had their choice of life in prison here at Hotel California or being sent back to Texas to get fried like catfish."

"They didn't like the catfish idea?"

"I guess some people have more regard for their own skins than they do for the lives of others."

"So you didn't have to testify?"

Rachel smiled broadly and shook her head. It was the first time I'd seen her smile like that and it seemed like all the baggage she'd been carrying around was gone. It occurred to me that I'd never seen her this happy, she'd been living with her past as long as I'd known her.

"How have you been?" I asked.

"I'm going back to school."

"School?"

"Law school," she said. "The prosecutor's office is going to help me and they said I'd have a job with them when I graduate. I start this fall."

"That's great!"

She smiled and looked down. "Yeah, thanks."

"Listen, I'm on my way out," I said, taking my credit card from Stan. "We've got somebody trying to bring something into the harbor that we want to keep out of our fair city."

"It's a little too late for that, Jared," she said. "There's nothing they can bring in that's not already here."

"You're probably right," I said.

Rachel pressed a key into the palm of my hand. "Put this on your key ring," she said. "That way you won't have to leave a note on my door, you can come inside and wait for me."

Rachel pulled me close and kissed me on the cheek.

"What was that for?" I asked.

"Just saying thanks."

"For what?"

"I don't know. Being there. Saving my life. Understanding me." Rachel put her hand on my forearm and smiled. "I've gotta run now, I'm late for my protecting and serving gig."

"Protect and serve," I said as she left the bar. "Somebody's gotta do it."

The evening humidity assaulted me as soon as I stepped outside the air-conditioned bar. A string of trucks began pulling out of the China Line shipping terminal across the street.

"Forgive yourself," I said, repeating Reverend Johnny's words under my breath.

The bottle of pills in my hand sounded like my old friend the rattlesnake when I shook it, just before I lobbed it in front of one of the trucks. The first truck missed it and the bottle rolled over near the curb. Panic swept over me. What was I thinking? As soon as I started through the evening traffic on Harbor Boulevard for my pills, I saw the second truck run over it and then there was nothing left but plastic shards and white powder.

"Forgive yourself today or you won't be able to function tomorrow," Reverend Johnny had said.

Forgive myself? I'm not there yet. I'm still trying to be honest with myself.

The end

About the Author

Alex Clifford spent over twenty-five years in the United States Merchant Marine and is a veteran of the Vietnam War. He now resides in Montana, where in addition to writing, he raises Tennessee Walking Horses and trains bird dogs.